K is the ~~bes~~... ~~ne~~
Murderous Maths series and many
other books, most of which were
illustrated by Philip Reeve. He was born and
lives in York and has a wife, four daughters
and about 1300 copies of the *Beano*.

PHILIP REEVE

worked in a bookshop for many
years before breaking out and
becoming an illustrator. He is also
the award-winning author of the
Mortal Engines quartet. Philip now lives on
Dartmoor with his wife, Sarah, and their son
Samuel.

URGUM
AND THE
SEAT
OF FLAMES

Kjartan Poskitt illustrated by Philip Reeve

SCHOLASTIC

First published in the UK in 2007 by Scholastic Children's Books
An imprint of Scholastic Ltd
Euston House, 24 Eversholt Street
London, NW1 1DB, UK
Registered office: Westfield Road, Southam, Warwickshire, CV47 0RA
SCHOLASTIC and associated logos are trademarks and or registered trademarks of
Scholastic Inc.

Text copyright © Kjartan Poskitt, 2007
Cover and inside illustrations © Philip Reeve, 2007
The rights of Kjartan Poskitt and Philip Reeve to be identified as the author and
illustrator of this work have been asserted by them.

10 digit ISBN 1 407 10433 0
13 digit ISBN 978 1407 10433 1

Printed in the UK by CPI Bookmarque, Croydon, CR0 4TD
Papers used by Scholastic Children's Books are made from wood grown in
sustainable forests.

3 5 7 9 10 8 6 4

www.scholastic.co.uk/zone

For Bridget and
our four Mollys

CONTENTS

THE PROLOGUE:

PART ONE

THE BOUNTY HUNTER

PART TWO

THE BATTLE MARKET

PART THREE

THE SAVVY AWARDS

THE EPILOGUE:

The Prologue:
The Blue Feather

The pale blue feather slowly twisted and fluttered all the way down from the high rocky path and landed neatly in the girl's lap. It was long and ragged, greasy and matted with filth and she was delighted to see it. She had been sitting on the parched ground for ages with nothing but seven bored horses and a curious selection of old leather bags for company. She had ignored the odd scraps of clothing, armour, hair, finger and all the other usual stuff that had been falling all around her, but the feather was far more interesting. She picked it up, screwing up her nose in distaste. It certainly hadn't come from any bird that she'd ever seen in the Lost Desert. For one thing it was *so* filthy that no bird would ever have managed to fly with it, even Djinta and Percy, her pet vultures, who were circling high above, kept themselves tidier than this. And it really was the *most* revolting pale blue colour, a bit like deeply sour hippopotamus milk.

She looked up to see where it had come from, but there was no clue. Just the endless blast of cheers, screams, whoops and bashes echoing down from where her father and brothers were ambushing a bunch of wandering savages who had strayed too close to home.

WALLOP
KERRUNCH
OOYAH
BIFF SCROLTCH

They had been at it for ages, and as usual they had left her and her brother Raymond to guard the horses and miss the fun. She sighed and looked at the feather again. There was a small glob of blood at the end to show it had been freshly ripped from whatever it had been growing on. Just as the girl was starting to imagine what the complete bird must look like, the horses started to shift uneasily. They were backing away from the rock face as a strange shadow appeared on the sand. Once again the girl looked up, shielding her eyes from the glare of the overhead sunlight, and tried to make sense of what she saw. Something was scrambling down the cliff towards her. Every so often it would lose its grip but instead of plummeting to the ground it seemed to swoop around and steer itself to crash back into the cliff side again.

"What is it?" asked a voice from one of the bags.

"I don't know," said the girl.

Even when it hit the ground …

FAB-BLAMM

… in front of the bemused horses, she still didn't know what it was. But at least she had found out where the feather had come from.

The creature staggered to an upright position, and it turned out to be not much taller than the girl herself. From under its battered metal armour the girl could see many more revolting pale blue feathers sticking out. Its head had big flappy human ears, long wispy black hair and what looked like a very big (in fact *very*, very big) curved nose. It had small arms and hands, one of which was clutching a curved blade, and on its feet it had … well, actually it didn't have feet, they were more like big hands. The girl wasn't too surprised, after all there had been some very strange creatures appearing in the Lost Desert recently, but even without the feathers, this had to be the strangest. The creature's tiny black eyes stared at the girl, then it cocked its head to one side.

"Don't stop me, don't stop me," it said. The big nose thing seemed to have split open at the bottom and what looked like a lumpy black sausage was dangling out. It was at that point the girl real-ized the curved nose was actually a beak, and the dangly thing was the creature's tongue.

"I won't," she said and meant it. She had no intention of going near the thing, whatever it was.

"Who's a good girl then?" it said. "Who's a good girl?"

The creature hopped around on its huge hand-feet and hurried towards the horses, who watched it with bored interest. The creature launched itself at the biggest horse and clawed its way up on to its back.

"Oy!" shouted the girl, leaping to her feet. "You be careful of that horse. He's not yours, so get off."

"Make me," said the creature with a nasty cackle.

"Can't be bothered," said the girl. "Suit yourself. If you want to stay there, stay there."

"Ha!" shouted the creature. "Giddy up, horsey. Giddy up, horsey."

But the horsey didn't giddy up. It looked at the girl for advice, and she shook her head. No giddy up, the message was clear enough. That suited the horse fine. This creature thing seemed to have a lot of spiky bones digging into him and the big fingers on the end of its stumpy legs that were grabbing into his sides were most uncomfortable. The other horses had sauntered over in a gesture of sympathy, and they all rubbed their noses together and thought of nice things like flowers to eat and stripy poles to jump over.

"GIDDY UP, HORSEY!" shouted the creature.

Once again the horse looked over to the girl. If he really had to giddy up then he would, but he hoped he didn't have to. Luckily, the girl was there to make the right decision for him.

"Why should he giddy up?" said the girl. "You'll only ride him until he drops and leave him somewhere he doesn't want to be."

The other horses nodded in agreement. She was right. That was exactly the sort of thing that happened to horses. The horses liked the girl. She understood what it was to be a horse, even though she was a girl. Maybe the girl liked eating flowers and jumping over stripy poles, but they weren't certain about that. That's because they were horses and she was a girl. At least they were certain about that. The horses all nodded again.

PING BLATT *puff pant* TINKY-TONK *wheeze* PLOP *gasp* DINK

Judging by the sounds, the fight was coming to an end. The girl looked up and saw the vultures were circling lower to see what was dead enough to eat.

"Robbin will be coming down soon," she said. "That's his horse, so I'd get off it if I were you."

The creature was starting to panic. Clearly the horse wasn't going to go anywhere unless the girl said it could, and therefore the girl had to be dealt with. Leaping down to the ground it scurried towards her holding its blade out in front. Although it couldn't actually walk very quickly, every so often a pair of very tatty unfit wings flapped out from its back and it managed a long swooping jump.

The girl realized the creature could catch her, and had already dashed around to the other side of a large flat dip in the ground.

"Behave yourself," she said. "Or Raymond will have to teach you some manners."

"Raymond, who's Raymond?" asked the creature, coming to a stop. "Raymond, who's Raymond?"

Without moving its body, the creature turned its head almost all the way round and back again. It couldn't see anyone else apart from the horses and the girl. The only other things that weren't sand or rock were a set of dusty old leather bags next to where it was standing. The girl was bluffing! She had to be bluffing, but she was doing it well because she didn't look in the least scared. Her hands loosely rested on her hips and she had one eyebrow raised in a totally unimpressed manner.

"Come here!" screeched the creature. It braced itself to leap across the dip in the sand. "I'll get you, and then you'll get me out of here!"

The creature took a step backwards, spread its tatty

wings, then took a jump. A leg stuck out of one of the bags, neatly tripped it up and the creature fell beak first on to the dip in the ground. The thin cloth underneath the shallow layer of sand ripped apart and the creature fell down the hole into the pool of sloppy tar at the bottom.

SPER-LUDGE

The girl looked down. The creature was making enough noise to show that it wasn't too badly hurt, but it was completely stuck.

"I warned you about Raymond," said the girl. "But you wouldn't listen. He's been living in the bags ever since a razor snake cut him into forty-seven pieces."

"Never mind him. Somebody should have warned me about you!" The eyes were blinking rapidly and, now it had given up trying to pull itself out of the tar, the creature was overtaken by curiosity. "Who, who are you?"

"Me?" asked the girl. "Me, I'm Molly. How do you do?"

"Molly? Never heard of you!"

"Oh, I'm nobody really," she admitted as a glow of pride crossed her face. "But you might of heard of my dad. He's Urgum the Axeman."

PART ONE:

The Bounty Hunter

REWARD

The Wifiest Wife

Urgum the Axeman was the fiercest savage the Lost Desert had ever known. He was very big, very strong and very, very smelly and proud of it. He lived in a cave with his wife and his seven savage sons and he spent his days happily charging around the desert fighting and eating, sometimes both at the same time. It was a satisfying and simple life, or at least it was most of the time.

Occasionally it got complicated, such as the time when Urgum went away for a few days and got back to find he had a ten-year-old daughter. (The gods of the Lost Desert can make a few days ten years long when they want to.) Urgum was very fond of his daughter, even if she did complicated daughterish things such as catching a blue-feathered hand-footed creature and keeping it in the bear pit and feeding it bananas like she'd done yesterday. But most of Urgum's complications came from his wife Divina.

Although Urgum was the fiercest savage the Lost Desert had ever known, Divina was the wifiest wife the Lost Desert had ever known. Divina never charged around the desert picking fights with as many people as possible at once, she never played silly games such as who can fit the most porcupines down their trousers and she certainly never ate anyone to death. The reason

Divina didn't indulge in the traditional savage pastimes was that she was the daughter of one of the rich soft-hand families that lived and worked in the fabulous Laplace Palace. Divina despised the rich, lazy softhand life, and so when she and Urgum first got married, she had abandoned everything to live in Urgum's cave, and had provided him with his seven savage sons without a word of complaint. (Well, obviously she'd shoved his dinner in his face a few times, and dropped his favourite axe down the toilet hole… **PAD-DINK-A-DANKY-SPLUDDOOSH** … and on the odd occasion she'd set fire to his feet when he was asleep, but no words of complaint. Words of complaint were what softhands tried to frighten each other with, but it didn't work with savages. If you went up to a savage and folded your arms and stuck your nose up and said, "I intend to lodge a strongly worded complaint about you," by the time the words reached the savage's ears, somehow they would have changed into "I'm a whining little snot, so please punch me on the hooter." Divina knew this and respected it. That's why she never uttered a word of complaint. And besides, dropping an axe down the toilet hole is a lot more fun because it goes **PAD-DINK-A-DANKY-SPLUD-DOOSH.**)

Of course it hadn't been easy starting life as a soft-hand and then going off to live in a cave with savages, but Divina had done it and survived. It had taken guts, trickery, sarcasm, a sense of humour, an extremely frightening left eyebrow and enough attitude to make a charging rhinoceros back off and take up knitting. That's why Divina was the wifiest wife that the Lost Desert had ever known.

One Simple Little Job

It was early morning in the kitchen at the back of Urgum's cave. Urgum's biggest son Robbin had gone out to grab a couple of ostriches while Divina was poking the fire. Urgum was helping by standing in the corner dribbling.

"We've nearly run out of firewood," said Divina.

"Never mind," said Urgum. "I like raw ostrich."

"Well you might," snapped Divina, "but I don't!"

"If you're going to be fussy you can pull the feathers out first," said Urgum.

"Urgum!" snapped Divina. "Go and get some logs and be back soon!"

It all sounded simple enough, so Urgum grabbed his axe and set out to get some logs and be back soon. It was a boring job, but being snapped at by Divina was even more boring and the only other thing he could think of doing was hiding down the toilet hole all day so she couldn't snap at him, but that would have been the *most* boring. Poor old Urgum. When he was younger there used to be lots of exciting things he could choose to do, but these days he found himself having to choose what the least boring thing was and today it was chopping logs. Boring boring boring.

Urgum's cave entrance was just one of several dotted around the inner walls of Golgarth Cragg, which was a big rock basin that only had one way in and out through a large crack in the wall. Over on the other side of the basin his oldest and ugliest friend, Mungoid the Ungoid, was sitting on a rock outside his own cave.

"Fancy coming to get some logs?" shouted Urgum, waving his axe.

"I'm a bit busy right now," said Mungoid.

Just then, a tall savage in tight skirmish armour stepped out of the cave next to Mungoid and flicked her long flame-red hair away from her face. As she put an arrow to the bow she was carrying, a much smaller and completely hair-covered savage dashed out and stood next to her, holding out a large metal pan. The tall savage

raised the bow over her head and fired the arrow
straight upwards.

"Good morning, Grizelda!" said Mungoid,
licking his hand and smoothing down the three
hairs that stuck out of the top of his head.

FWEEE – DANK!

An eagle dropped straight into the
pan with the arrow through the
middle of its head.

"Another perfect shot!" said
Mungoid admiringly.

The tall savage glanced at
him. She didn't smile, but she
didn't not smile either. With
another flick of her hair,
she disappeared into her
cave, followed by the little
savage with the pan.
Mungoid sighed happily

and *twink plink dink* the three hairs on his head shot up again. He got to his feet.

"Right then," he said. "Logs!"

"And we have to be back soon," said Urgum.

"That sounds simple enough," said Mungoid. "The Wandering Jungle's stopped for a rest just outside the Cragg. So logs, soon, no problem."

Urgum and Mungoid set off across the basin to the crack in the cragg wall where, as always, Olk, the giant Guardian of Golgarth, was standing on guard.

Olk's massive sword was slung across his shoulder, and as they passed under it they realized they had better check that they knew the password to get back in.

"Enormous-strawberry-fool-ice-cream," they said together. Very slowly Olk's neck bent and straightened again. He'd nodded, so they'd got the password right. Phew! It wasn't exactly their choice of password, but as Divina was the only person that Olk ever took orders from, they'd let her choose it. Mind you, it was a good password. Who'd ever guess that?

So all they had to do now was get some logs and be back soon. The important words were *logs* and *soon* and just to make sure they didn't forget what they were supposed to be doing, as they marched along they repeated "log-soon … logsoon … logsoon …"

What could be simpler? That was early in the morning.

The Dreaded Gap

Late that afternoon, Divina was sitting at her dressing table admiring all her tubs of powder, coloured face paints, sniffy stuff, fancy bottles full of mysterious yuk, combs, brushes, necklaces, bracelets, anklets, fingerlets, toelets, noselets, tummybuttonlets and so on, when she was horrified to see something on it that she'd never seen before. It was an empty gap. Eeek!

Divina's dressing table was very important to her. Whenever she got fed up of Urgum and the boys rolling home covered in blood, laughing their heads off and comparing their new scars, she'd go and sit at her dressing table. She'd tinker with her bits and pieces and read *Modern Savage* magazine and lose her mind in a world where everything looked fabulous and smelt gorgeous and tasted of strawberry fool ice cream.

The gap hadn't been there when she'd first sat down, but as she was combing her hair, something on the table had twitched. She hadn't really seen it before as it had been tucked behind a tall bottle of something special that she was saving for something special. The twitchy thing was like a grey potato, but then an eye opened on the side. It pulled its two long legs out of its mouth and breathed out, which made it shrink down to the size of a skinny nothing. It stood up, licked its lips and hopped off the table and away. It was one of the desert's odder little creatures. You could look at it, but unless it moved, you could never actually *notice* it.

"A gap-filler!" sighed Divina. "It must have been there for ages, and now it's left … a gap!"

Divina hated gaps on her dressing table. In her old softhand days, a gap was an excuse to go out and get something fabulously exquisite to put in it, and just because Divina was living in a cave with a bunch of bloodthirsty savages, she saw no reason to let her standards drop. Unfortunately, although Urgum could provide her with huge dripping chunks of animal to eat and skins to wear, he wasn't very good at bringing home fabulously exquisite things, or indeed any other sort of thing that didn't need chopping with his axe. That meant that if Divina wanted something fabulously exquisite, she needed money to buy it, and that's when things got extra complicated.

Urgum hated money. Occasionally he'd return with something that she could sell at the market, such as a pair of earrings (probably with the ears still attached), but to Urgum money itself was just little round bits of metal that were too small to hit anyone with, and tasted horrible. All anyone seemed to do with money was count it, and as Urgum could only count up to one, he didn't think that money was any fun at all.

Divina looked at the gap again and felt all itchy. She shuffled the things round until the gap was at the front of the table, then she put her *Modern Savage* magazine over it. It didn't work. When you're filling dressing-table gaps, magazines just don't count. But then Divina spotted a picture followed by a big notice:

REWARD! WANTED DEAD OR ALIVE*
(*Preferably dead, but if it's alive then hopefully it's well tied up and has been given a good thumping.)

Divina gasped in excitement. At last, she'd found something that Urgum could actually do and get paid for! He was good at bringing things home dead (or alive, tied up and having been given a good thumping). The only tricky bit was that nobody in their right mind would ever dare tell the fiercest savage in the Lost Desert that he had to go and do something for money. Well, nobody that is apart from the wifiest wife in the Lost Desert. Divina knew she just needed to find exactly the right moment, the sort of moment when Urgum was a bit in trouble, a bit apologetic, a bit sheepish … in fact, the sort of moment that's coming up right now.

Exactly the Right Moment

Divina had been waiting all day for Urgum to get some logs for the breakfast fire and be back soon, but surprise surprise, things hadn't quite gone to plan. After Urgum and Mungoid had passed Olk, they had only had to walk a short distance saying "logsoon … logsoon …" before they reached the massive, heaving, dripping, squawking Wandering Jungle. So far so good, but when they got there, they bumped into a few savage friends who had just invented a marvellous reason for a completely pointless fight. They had all been having a "who-can-find-the-bentest-twig-competition?" and naturally when Krunz accused Ffarg of twisting his twig to make it look bendier, Ffarg smashed his fist into Krunz's jaw, then everybody grabbed their mallets, swords, clubs and razor chains and piled in. Urgum and Mungoid hurriedly found some bent twigs of their own, accused everybody else of cheating and were soon in the middle of the action. It was evening before they staggered back to the cragg, each of them still holding their bent twig, each of them still muttering "logsoon … logsoon …" and each of them wishing that they were each other. Mungoid just had an empty cave to go back to, he wished there was somebody waiting for him, but there wasn't. Urgum had a full cave to go back to, he wished there was no one waiting for him, but there was.

It had been a super fight, but Urgum hadn't really enjoyed it because he knew that Divina had been expecting "logsoon" since the early morning. Urk! She was his lovely wife, who spent her days looking after his sons and daughter and keeping everything nice and comfortable for them all and NEVER ASKING ANYTHING IN RETURN, and yet when he was given ONE SIMPLE LITTLE JOB like nipping out to fetch a bit of firewood all he could do was stagger back far too late, dripping with sweat and blood and clutching one bent twig. Urgum was already bracing himself for the deadly sarcastic lecture about responsibility and reliability and accountability and sensibility and probably a few extra bilities that Divina would make up to confuse him. He knew he deserved it, but to make things slightly easier for him Mungoid handed him his own bent twig. At least if Urgum turned up with two twigs, he might not be in so much trouble as if he just had one twig. And so it was that Urgum approached his cave muttering "twigslate … twigslate …" hoping that Divina wouldn't notice the difference.

By the time he got home, Divina was back in the kitchen where their biggest son Robbin had helped her shove a couple of ostriches on to a long metal skewer over the fire. The ostriches had put up a good struggle with giant claws and feathers flying everywhere, but at last they were in place with their heads dangling down and their big eyes blinking in puzzlement at the tiddly little flame below them. The ostriches had been there nearly all day and were starting to wonder if they would die of old age before they were cooked.

"Did you get some more firewood, Dad?" asked Robbin when Urgum arrived. "Otherwise breakfast that became lunch that's now supposed to be tea will have to be breakfast tomorrow."

"Of course," said Urgum, trying to sound confident. "This lot should hot things up a bit." He threw the two blood-spattered twigs on the fire then sat down beside it, rubbed his hands together and held them out as if to feel the wafts of extra heat. Would Divina notice they weren't logs? Robbin certainly noticed and hurried out of the kitchen. Although Robbin was a huge, fierce and merciless savage who enjoyed shoving live ostriches on long metal skewers, he was also a sensitive soul and he hated watching his mother turning his father into a sorrowful jelly.

Urgum braced himself. *Here it comes*, he thought, already feeling apologetic and sheepish.

"Well done, dear," said Divina.

Well done? Urgum looked at the little spluttering flame and the two grinning ostriches. Maybe she hadn't noticed after all? Wow! He discreetly put his hand over the new hole in his vest where he'd been gouged with

29

a spiked trowel. Divina was never one to admire a new hole in a vest or even a decent scar for that matter, but maybe she wouldn't notice that either!

"That's a pretty one, dear!" she said, watching the blood seep through his fingers. "It's not often they put one on you!"

She HAS noticed, thought Urgum. *Oooooooops!* All he could do was wait for his worst thing, when she raised her extremely frightening left eyebrow. That was the sign that the long words would start and he'd end up gibbering away pointless apologies and sheepish lies that he'd never do it again.

"I've got something to show you," said Divina, picking up her copy of *Modern Savage*. "Look, you'll like it."

Urgum gulped. How could he like anything in *Modern Savage* magazine? Oh dear, today's sarcastic lecture was starting to bite already and she hadn't even raised her eyebrow yet. Was his punishment going to be designer socks or a lilac hairband? Of course when she pointed at the notice, the letters on the page meant nothing to Urgum, but when she explained that there was a reward for capturing the toughest, meanest, filthiest savage in the desert, Urgum started to realize that she actually wasn't being sarcastic. What's more, Divina was smiling at him. She was right, he DID like it!

"Wow!" he said. "A reward? That's fantastic!"

Divina was relieved. Even though she knew she'd got Urgum in his apologetic and sheepish mode, she hadn't been sure if it would be enough to control him when she told him he had to get paid money by softhands.

"Good old *Modern Savage* magazine!" said Urgum. "Thanks to them, lots of little saddos hoping to make some softhand money will be coming to get me!"

"You?" gasped Divina.

"Of course, ME! I'm the toughest, meanest, filthiest savage in the desert!"

"Er ... actually that's not quite what it says ..."

"It doesn't matter what it says, I know what it means! I'll get all the fighting I could ever want, all fresh and eager and queuing up on the doorstep."

"Urgie!" said Divina. "Look at the picture."

Urgum wasn't one for spending much time in front of mirrors, so he wasn't exactly sure what he looked like. But he was exactly sure what he DIDN'T look like and he was looking at it. "That's not me!" he choked. "That's ... that's a nappar! What's that ugly, long, gibbering streak of snot doing there?"

"That's who they want dead or alive," said Divina.

WANTED

DEAD OR ALIVE

THE TOUGHEST, MEANEST FILTHIEST SAVAGE IN THE LOST DESERT

BY ORDER:

"A FLIPPIN' NAPPAR?" shouted Urgum. "Tough? Mean? FILTHY?"

"Yes, dear," said Divina, "but don't you see, this is very good for us!"

"It's unfair!" sulked Urgum. "Look at me! I'm a lot tougher than any nappars! And I'm meaner. And filth? I'll show them who's filthy! I've got more filth in my belly button than a gang of nappars could shovel over a cliff in a day."

"I know that," said Divina, trying not to think of Urgum's belly button. "But there's a tribe of them and they've been attacking softhands. That's why they want them catching."

"Attacking softhands?" scoffed Urgum. "What's tough about that? You can tell your softhands from me that if nappars are attacking them, that's not tough, that's deeply sad. I'd be embarrassed to be seen attacking soft-hands. I tell you, the toughest savage in the desert is standing right here and you're married to him. And as a lucky bonus you just happen to be married to the meanest and filthiest savage too. If you don't believe me I'll show you my belly button."

"Don't show me, show them!"

"That sounds fun. I'll smash my way into *Modern Savage* magazine and show them my belly button. Hah! That'll show them."

"No, no!" said Divina. "I mean show them how tough you are. All you have to do is get the nappars. You can do that, can't you?"

"Nappars?" scoffed Urgum. "Oh please. Getting nappars would be like going on a picnic."

"Lovely! Then you can go and pick up the reward."

"Reward? So what is this reward anyway?"

"Oh, whatever …" said Divina, trying to be casual. "I hadn't really looked, being softhands it'll just be some money, I expect …"

"Money? Softhand money? I HATE MONEY!"

Urgum was just about to explode when, luckily for Divina there was a strange noise from the fireplace. One of the ostriches had managed to blow the little flame out …

PFFF-THS

… and the other was having an upside-down ostrich laugh …

"PNOOP PNOOP PNOOP."

"The fire's gone out," said Divina. "By the way, wasn't it your job to get some logs? Soon?"

The eyebrow was up and she was taking a deep breath. Eeek!

"Don't change the subject!" said Urgum. "As I was saying, I'm the toughest meanest filthiest savage in the desert and if I have to get a reward to prove it to you then I will."

Urgum stomped out of the kitchen feeling very smug that he'd wriggled out of the logsoon problem, and completely unaware that he'd just been completely outwriggled by the wifiest wife the Lost Desert had ever known.

Divine Disgust

Urgum wasn't the only person who was unsure about him getting rewards from softhands. High up beyond the sky were the Hallowed Halls of Sirrus, where all the different gods of the Lost Desert lived. The gods were so powerful that they could squash mountains and spin up storms, but at the same time they were extremely delicate because they relied on people believing in them. If a god ran out of believers, then quite simply it would stop being a god and become just another formless whisper drifting aimlessly through the sky for eternity. It was a worrying thought and one which was never far from the minds of the twin barbarian gods, Tangor and his sister, Tangal.

"We can't have Urgum getting paid money by soft-hands!" said Tangal in horror. "He's our last true barbarian believer; if we lose him we've had it!"

"It's only a reward," said Tangor, trying to reassure them both. "It's just the once. He'd be ashamed to find himself making a habit of it."

"Let's hope so," said Tangal. "If he gets tempted into

wages then next it'll be holiday pay, sickness benefits, he might even end up …"

"No, don't say it!"

"… in a pension scheme!"

They stared at each other in horror. True barbarians only ate what they killed, they slept on rocks and most importantly, they died gloriously and gruesomely. Surely their last believer was far too proud to be lured away by the accountancy gods? Thanks to those purple-tied, novelty-cufflinked, potted-plant-watering freaks, many of the nastiest savages in the desert had quietly forgotten what it was to be a fearless, thrill-seeking, death-defying warrior and were now sitting out their old age getting excited about tax-free annuity dividends.

"The trouble is that the whole desert's getting softer," said Tangal. "There's no decent fights left and he's getting bored silly."

"But he had quite a good fight with his friends when he went to get logs with Mungoid," said Tangor.

"You call that a good fight?" Tangal stared at her brother, her eyes wide with disgust. "They all stopped and went home for tea! How sad's that? Urgum needs reminding that a *real* fight should be a matter of life and death."

Tangor nodded. "You're right. Urgum needs a real fight, it'll give him the buzz of being a champion again. He won't get that fighting for little rewards."

"For a real fight he needs a real enemy," said Tangal thoughtfully. "Something strong …"

"… nasty …"

"… cunning …"

"… something he hates so much that he has to kill them or die trying …"

"… but what?"

The divine twins groaned in frustration. Urgum had faced up to giant eagles and six-headed bulls, even on his wedding day he'd chewed the tail off a unicorn. What else could they send him to fight? Whatever it was, they had to think of it fast before he lost interest in extreme hardship and continuous danger and slipped into a world of beige socks, warm milky drinks and maybe even … *gulp* … soap.

Beauty and the Bait

All the richest softhands lived at the fabulous Laplace Palace, which had perfume spas, sporting arenas, flowers, minstrels, mime artists, libraries, huge comfy sofas, restaurants that served teeny-weeny meals on ridiculously big plates, statues, baskets of rotten fruit to throw at mime artists, dress shops and acrobatic giraffes. In fact, it had everything a softhand could possibly want apart from one thing, it didn't have poor people for the softhands to show their money off in front of. (Of course there were thousands of slaves, servants and other assorted workers, but softhands don't count them as people.)

That's why every so often the softhands felt obliged to escape the grinding monotony of unlimited luxury and venture to one of the surrounding setttlements. There they could display their clothes and jewellery, and enjoy the fun of accidentally dropping the money when they paid for things, so that the poorer people had to get on the floor and pick it up.

One of the main tracks from Laplace Palace led through the Unsightly Hills of Nap. Nappars were the gangly scum of the Lost Desert, so it was no wonder that passing softhand convoys could suddenly find themselves surrounded by tall gibbering bandits, and soon they'd be heading home again without their jewels, coats, false teeth and usually with their pants stuffed in their mouths to stop them whingeing about it. Of course, the softhands had sent out squadrons of guardslaves to round the nappars up, but they were no match for the lanky savages with their nasty little pointed swords. That's why, to the softhands' disgust, they'd had to rely on a savage answer to a savage problem.

Urgum knew that fighting nappars was easy enough, the problem was getting hold of them. With their ridiculously long arms and legs, nappars could creep across the jagged rocks faster than any other savage, or any horse or monkey or even the new eight-legged spider-goat for that matter. Chasing them was pointless, so what Urgum needed was a bait to catch the nappars, and he had the perfect idea.

It was the morning after the "logsoon" episode and the seven savage sons were still asleep. With a big smirk on his face Urgum crept along the cave passage to their room. "WAKEY WAKEY," he shouted and threw a handful of rattlesnakes in through the doorway.

FRITTER SNITTER HISSSS.

"Yag!" "Urgh!" "Eek!" shouted the seven savage sons, leaping up from their beds and charging out past him. As always, Ruff, the eldest and shortest, was first, followed by the skinny one Ruinn, then came the twins Rekk 'n' Rakk, and then Robbin, who had paused to collect the bags that contained Raymond. Oh, and then the seventh son came last, but nobody noticed.

Soon they were all gathered outside the cave, blinking in the white desert sunlight.

"I need a volunteer for a very special job," Urgum announced. "It's dangerous, stupid and there's a very good chance you'll be killed. So who's up for it?"

The sons immediately rubbed their eyes and woke up properly. This sounded like fun, so long as it was somebody else that volunteered.

"I'd love to do it, but I better not," said Ruff. "After all,

I am the number one son, I am the leader, and without me the others won't have anyone to look up to."

"We don't look up to you anyway, shorty," said Ruinn.

"So we'll volunteer you," said Rekk and Rakk.

"Big cheer for the volunteer!" said Ruinn.

"Hooray!" they all cheered.

"Good lad," said Urgum. He put a proud fatherly hand on Ruff's shoulder, spun him round, and then with a proud fatherly boot up the bottom he sent his number one son flying back into the cave.

WHUMP!

From inside the cave came some suspicious girlie giggling. "Oh no you don't!" screamed Ruff's voice. "GET OFF! STOP THAT! NO WAY!"

"Oooh!" said all the others when Ruff finally stepped outside again. He was wearing Divina's wedding dress, which was about twice as big as he was. Divina and Molly were walking behind holding the long white lace skirt up to stop it getting caught.

"If I hear even just one tiny little laugh ..." said Ruff in a tough voice.

"HA HA HA HA HA HA HA HA," laughed six of the savage sons.

"RIGHT!" cursed Ruff. "Prepare to DIE HORRIBLY."

He launched himself at his brothers, but his feet got caught in the cloth and he rolled over and got completely bundled up like a giant snowball.

"HA HA HA HA HA HA HA HA," laughed six of the savage sons again.

"It's a good job you're all laughing," said Molly. "Because obviously Ruff's too small for the dress, and so am I. So one of you will have to wear it."

"Why?" they all gasped.

Urgum explained. "We need someone to look like a softhand, and your mum's wedding dress is the only softhand outfit we've got."

Molly helped Ruff crawl out of the tangled dress, then Divina lifted it up and fondly stroked the crusty old red and brown stains on it.

"What are those marks, Mum?" asked Molly.

"Blood and unicorn dung from the wedding," smiled Divina. "It was the happiest day of my life."

"If someone has to wear that dress, why can't it be Mum?" demanded Ruinn.

"Because since we got married she's got far too …" Urgum was just about to give the correct answer, when Divina's left eyebrow arched menacingly. "… many other things to do."

"Oh," said Ruinn. "I thought it was because she's got far too fat."

"Ex-*CUSE* me," said Divina in a voice that made Ruinn feel like he was having his teeth scraped with a knife. "It's the dress that's got slimmer, actually. In fact, I'd say it was exactly YOUR size."

"What?" gasped Ruinn. "That's not fair!"

"Well, one of you lot has to wear it," said Urgum.

"Then let's at least fight about it," said Ruinn. "Last one dead's the winner."

"I think Rekk should wear it!" shouted Rakk, pointing at his twin brother.

"No way!" shouted Rekk. "I'm not wearing it. YOU wear it!"

"But you'd look pretty in it!"

"I'll make you *pretty*!"

"I don't mind wearing it," said Robbin. "Are there hair ribbons too?"

So it was decided. Even though Robbin was quite a lot larger than Divina, once they'd got all his clothes off, somehow they managed to squeeze him into the dress. They did his hair up.

"Right then," said Urgum. "Me and Robbin are off to get a few nappars. You lot wait here."

"Yes, and don't get into trouble while we're out," said Divina.

Urgum's ear twitched. It had just heard something strange, something that shouldn't have been heard. It quickly rewound the last few words: "out – we're – while – trouble" and played them back "trouble while *we're* out" – that was it! The ear immediately set off the alarms in Urgum's brain.

"What do you mean *we're*?" demanded Urgum.

"I mean us," explained Divina. "We're going to get some nappars."

"WE aren't going to get any nappars," said Urgum. "It's just me, all by myself, alone, with Robbin, just the one of us, on my own."

Molly was dragging a wicker basket out of the cave.

"I've got the picnic, Mum," she said.

"What's this?" gasped Urgum.

"You said getting nappars was like going on a picnic," said Divina. "Molly's been looking forward to it."

"There's giraffe ribs and pelican wings," said Molly. "Come on, Dad, let's be off then."

"Absolutely un-no-not!" insisted Urgum. "Nappars are nasty dangerous things. I've enough to deal with without you two getting in the way."

"We'll stay back," said Divina. "You won't notice we're there. Cheer up, it'll be fun."

"THIS IS NOT GOING TO BE FUN," shouted Urgum.

"Oh come on, grumpy," smiled Divina. "How do you know until we've got there?"

Urgum had a bit more shouting to do, but it was too late. Divina, Molly and Robbin were already going to get their horses. All Urgum could do was follow, dragging his axe behind him and leaving the other boys laughing and whistling at his back.

On the other side of the rock basin, Grizelda the Grisly stepped out of her cave. She'd heard the whistles and knew it meant Urgum and his family were doing something ridiculous, but Grizelda hadn't time for that rubbish. With a flick of her head, she tossed her long locks of flame-coloured hair over her shoulders and let them cascade down her back. Sitting on a boulder outside the cave along from her was good old ugly Mungoid the Ungoid, who was staring across at the others.

Grizelda couldn't be bothered with men, but there had been one time when she and Mungoid had been in Urgum's kitchen and she had let him sit next to her for no special reason. It had turned out to be sort of nice and friendly and she'd never forgotten it, so maybe that was why, when she saw Mungoid sitting outside his cave, she decided to walk past him for no reason at all. Well, no reason apart from the fact that she'd just washed her hair and knew she looked gorgeous and, well … she just fancied walking past him, that's all. She knew he'd blush a bit, wipe his nose and say, "Good morning, Grizelda," and she wouldn't answer, and she wouldn't smile, but she wouldn't not smile either and then he'd be a bit confused and she'd feel good.

So Grizelda did her walk past, but to her astonishment, for once Mungoid didn't say anything. It was weird! Of course, Grizelda had to keep on walking as if she was going somewhere, but she sneaked a quick look back. Mungoid was *still* staring at the others. It was like he hadn't even seen her. How embarrassing was that?

Grizelda got as far as the entrance to the cragg and then, as she hadn't got much choice, she walked back to give Mungoid a second chance. She even slowed down as she went past him but ... nothing! She got back to her cave and felt very sour.

Urgum was also feeling sour. His rather brilliant nappar ambush had somehow turned into a family picnic, and to make things worse, when he went to get on his horse it was looking at him in a "not today, thanks" sort of way. Urgum's horse didn't like this fat sweaty man who made him gallop over crumbling rocks, leap across impossibly wide canyons and charge towards spears and cannons very much. It wouldn't have minded a little trot into the meadows to paddle through a pond or eat some flowers, but this had never happened before and it wasn't going to happen this time either. Fatty was walking towards him looking far too sour, and this meant that he would get himself into fighting mood by shouting, "Yarghhhh!" then running up and jumping on. Not surprisingly, the horse had got into the habit of taking a step to the side just as Fatty jumped, and there were a few joyful times when Fatty missed and landed in the dirt. But then Fatty had learnt to jump to the side at the last second, which meant that the horse had to stop taking a side step, and so Fatty would fly over the top and miss again (even more joy). Eventually they had got to the point where they each tried to guess what the other was going to do. Sometimes, the horse won (joy) and sometimes *OOOF!* Fatty won.

"YARGHHHH!" shouted Urgum.

To move or not to move? thought the horse. It quickly did a calculation involving speed of footsteps, softness of ground, wind direction and number of Fatty grunts, and at the last second it moved.

OOOOOF!

Urgum galloped off to join the others, feeling a bit better on a horse that was feeling a lot worse. Fatty might have beaten him this time, but somehow, some-time, somewhere, he'd get his revenge.

Meanwhile in her cave, Grizelda realized she'd have to be braver. Mungoid was still sitting and staring so she went out and stopped right in front of him.

"Hi," she said with super casualness.

"Yeah," said Mungoid, leaning over to peer around her. "Excuse me."

Mungoid was watching everybody riding out of the cragg, and in particular he was staring at the figure in the white dress.

"Are you all right?" asked Grizelda.

"Look, Urgum's got a new daughter!"

"What?" said Grizelda, rather taken aback.

"Oh wow!" said Mungoid, standing up and combing his hand over his three hairs. "And she is a beauty! I wonder where they're going?"

Unable to tear his eyes away, he hurried down to get

on his ox and follow. Luckily for Grizelda, her archer's eyesight was a lot better than the ungoid's. As she turned to go back inside, she was grinning so widely that she could hardly fit her face through the cave entrance.

The Thing in the Bear Pit

As Urgum, Divina and the others made their way to the Unsightly Hills of Nap, it got even more like a picnic because there was a whacking clap of thunder and heavy rains suddenly came plummeting down. If any of them had looked upwards they might have been surprised because it was still a cloudless sky and the sun was shining brightly.

Up in the hallowed Halls of Sirrus, the

barbarian gods were watching Urgum escorting his son in a dress out across the desert. Tangor had suddenly screamed with a thunderous roar, and his tears of shame had gone bucketing down to the ground.

"WHAT DOES URGUM THINK HE'S DOING?"

"Come on, maybe it's not that bad," said Tangal, trying to cheer her brother up. "Maybe the dress is a sign of toughness."

"What? Why? How?"

"Well … suppose you were a huge savage living in a desert full of other savages. What would be tougher – wearing your normal clothes or walking around wearing a dress?"

"By Zinko!" gasped Tangor. "Strange but true! You'd have to be pretty tough to wear a dress."

"Especially with hair ribbons," said Tangal.

"Oh no!" cried Tangor. "So does that mean Urgum should be wearing a dress and hair ribbons too? And how about … lipstick?"

Tangor wailed in anguish. Far below them the thunder crashed and rumbled and disturbed something in the bottom of the bear pit.

"Get a grip!" said Tangal, who was looking down at Golgarth Cragg, the happy scene of so many gruesome acts over the years. "That might suit some savages, but Urgum's still a barbarian. Like we said before, what he needs is a something to fight. Something nasty, cunning and horrible ... Hello, what's going on down there?"

GWARK!

The screech from the bear pit reached the cave where Urgum's other sons were sheltering. The rain had eased off, so they decided to go over and investigate. Down at the bottom of the pit, the blue-feathered creature that Molly had caught in her tar trap had been asleep on a pile of banana skins, but the thunder had woken it up and it wasn't happy to find itself soaking wet. In frustration, it was trying to jump up and claw its way out, but its stumpy little wings couldn't help it get high enough and the sides of the pit were too steep.

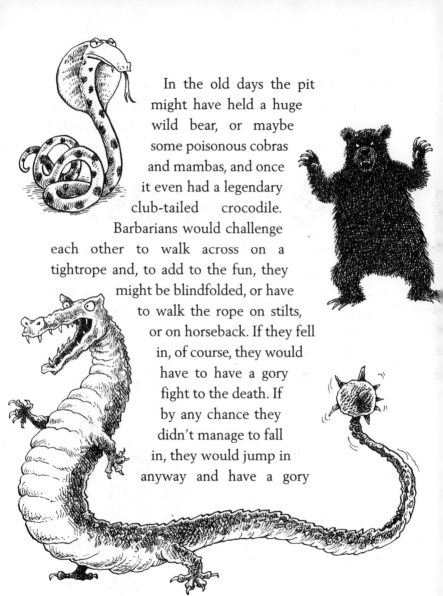

In the old days the pit might have held a huge wild bear, or maybe some poisonous cobras and mambas, and once it even had a legendary club-tailed crocodile. Barbarians would challenge each other to walk across on a tightrope and, to add to the fun, they might be blindfolded, or have to walk the rope on stilts, or on horseback. If they fell in, of course, they would have to have a gory fight to the death. If by any chance they didn't manage to fall in, they would jump in anyway and have a gory fight to the death. Jumping in was regarded as cheating, and so if you survived your fight to the death, everybody else would jump in and fight you to the death. The fun simply never stopped in the old days.

The tightrope was still there, but it was so worn through that in some places it was thinner than a single hair. Of course, a hair would never take a person's weight so anybody trying to get across just had to step over those bits.

GWARK!

"That thing's not happy!" laughed Ruinn, looking down. "Anybody fancy trying to walk across?"

"That would be a bit boring for me," said Ruff. "Too boring, in fact." He yawned a yawn of deep boredom, then picked up a stone and threw it down at the creature's head. The creature neatly snatched the stone out of the air, then hurled it straight back, catching Ruff – *schnitch* – on the nose.

"Yowch!" cried Ruff.

"Scaredy pants!" chanted Rekk and Rakk together.

"Scared?" said Ruff. "Me? Scared? Urgum the Axeman's number one favourite son? Ha! Even if I fell in, what's that thing going to do? It just looks like a fat bird with big ears, after all."

"You still look like a scaredy pants," said Ruinn.

"I don't look like a scaredy pants!" said Ruff. "Do I, Raymond?"

"I don't know what you look like," admitted Raymond, whose eyes were tied up in one of the bags. "But I can *smell* that you're a scaredy pants, Mr Scaredy Pants."

"Piffle!" said Ruff. "That thing can't scare me. All it can do is peel bananas with its feet. Just gimme a fork and I'd eat it to death."

"Prove it," said Ruinn.

"Well, I'd love to, but obviously I can't," said Ruff rather stupidly.

"Why not?" they all asked.

"Because I'm up here and it's down there. Duh!" (This was even more stupid.)

"You must be so disappointed," said Ruinn.

"Absolutely," said Ruff, breaking all previous records for extreme stupidity. "I just fancy a little snack."

That left the other sons with no more to be said.

WEEE-BLAMM!

The creature leapt out of the way as Ruff was thrown off the edge and hit the bottom of the pit. He struggled to his feet and tried to back into a corner, but he slipped on a banana skin and tumbled over backwards. From the other side of the pit the creature stared at him uncertainly.

"Ha ha ha!" laughed the boys from above.

"Shhh!" said Ruff, his lips and knees both trembling. "You might upset it!"

"I thought you were going to eat it," said Ruinn.

"I told you, I need a fork!" said Ruff desperately. "And a knife. And a sword. And a plate. And a napkin. And a club. And a shield. And …"

CLANKY BOYOING DUNK KER-PLINKY BASH

The boys threw the items into the pit. The creature ran its black tongue around its beak as it watched Ruff slither around on the banana skins desperately trying to grab everything. The one item that had fallen out of reach was the shield, and with a neat hop and a flutter the creature landed beside it, sat on its bottom and, with all four hands, held the shield up in front of its face.

"He's got the shield!" cried Ruff in panic.

"Never mind," said Ruinn. "You've got the fork and the plate. Don't forget to tell us what it tastes like."

"Mmmm!" said the creature admiring its reflection in the polished surface. "Pretty shiny thing. Pretty and shiny!"

Soon some violent sounds were echoing around the rock basin.

THUD
THUD
THUD

"What's happening?" asked Raymond's voice from inside a bag. "It sounds like Ruff's giving it a real bashing!"

"Not quite," replied Ruinn in amazement. "It's giving *itself* a real bashing."

Sure enough, as Ruff tripped and skidded around the bottom of the pit, the creature was happily banging its head against the shield.

"Mmm! Pretty and shiny!" it said.

Very slowly, Ruff crawled up behind it – he had the sword held high in his right hand, and the fork all ready for eating in his left hand. He was just about to strike, but the creature had seen his reflection in the shield. It spun round, grabbed Ruff round the throat and gave his head a quick bang on the shield, knocking him out cold. The creature grabbed the fork, held it over Ruff's nose and looked upwards.

"Get me out," it said. "Get me out or I eat him."

"You eat him!" cheered the boys together. "Hooray! Bye bye, Ruff."

They all set off back to the cave to burn Ruff's bed and divide his things up between them. The creature had to think quickly.

"Get me out, get me out," it shouted. "Or I *don't* eat him."

"Eh?" the boys said, hurrying back.

"You mean you're threatening to spare his life," gasped Ruinn in amazement. "You wouldn't!"

"What a dirty trick," said Rekk.

"We'll have to get it out!" said Rakk.

Moving at sulky teenager speed, Ruinn went to fetch a long knotted rope from the cave.

"We'll just have to say it escaped," said Rakk.

"And it's all Ruff's fault," said Rekk.

"Serves him right if he gets eaten," said Rakk.

"Ruff won't get eaten," said Raymond's voice from a bag.

"Why not?" said the others, disappointed.

"All it eats is bananas!"

"So what?" said Rekk. "Once the bird thing gets to the top we'll grab it and make it eat him. After all, Ruff's yellow and soft enough."

"Yeah!" said Rakk.

Ruinn had got back with the rope, so they lowered it down into the pit. The creature grabbed the end, but then it shot up it far faster than they expected, and with a flap of its filthy blue wings it flew right over their heads and landed on the ground behind them. The only person nearby was Raymond in his bags. His left arm stuck out and grabbed on to one of the short hairy legs, but the creature's strong hands twisted Raymond's arm round and round and round until it had to let go. Throwing the arm away, it bounded across the basin and disappeared through the cragg entrance.

"Olk's there," said Ruinn. "He'll stop it getting out."

Meanwhile, Raymond's arm crawled and flipped its way back to its bag, which Ruinn was holding open.

"Wow," said Ruinn to another bag, which had Raymond's ears in it. "You're lucky your arm was already off your body."

"Why?" said Raymond.

"Because otherwise he'd have twisted it off, right off your body."

"Oh, lucky me indeed," said Raymond.

From the bottom of the pit came a low groan as Ruff woke up.

"Has it gone?" he said nervously.

"Yeah," said Ruinn.

"Oh, pity," said Ruff, who then decided to try and break his own personal best for stupidity. "I could just do with a snack."

"Don't you worry about that!" shouted Rekk.

"We're going to get it back and throw it in again," said Rakk.

"Oh no!" said Ruff.

"OH YES!" cheered the boys as they dashed to the cragg entrance.

When they got there Olk was standing as still as ever and there was no sign of the creature. Surely Olk hadn't let it escape? They stepped past him and looked down Smiley Alley, the long row of stakes in the ground stretching off into the distance, each with a skull on the top. No sign of it. They looked up the steep cragg wall, right up to where the spiked boulders were balanced along the top. No sign. They dashed over to see if there were any blue feathers floating on top of the tar pit. No. They looked over towards the Wandering Jungle. Had the creature already got that far? They were just setting off to look when a low bubbly noise came from behind them. It came from deep within the great gut of the Golgarth Guardian. Something unusual was passing down the tubes, causing the digestive acids to react with a series of minor internal explosions.

"Olk?" asked Ruinn suspiciously. "Did you see where the bird thing went?"

With the speed and warmth of a sunrise, a massive grin slowly spread across Olk's face. Then his lips parted.

"BULRECHHH!"

The belch was so loud that Djinta and Percy, the two vultures perched high on the top of the cragg, almost tumbled from their nests. A single light blue feather fluttered out of the great mouth.

"Tasty!" said Olk.

Back up in the Halls of Sirrus there was huge excitement.

"It definitely stirs my gravy!" said Tangor. "Horrible, nasty, cunning …"

"Just a shame it wasn't bigger and stronger," said Tangal. "A few of those round the place would stop Urgum piddling about with nappars and money."

"Yeah, they'd remind him what barbarians are supposed to be about!" said Tangor gleefully. "But what was it?"

"Well, at a guess it was a chimpanzee-budgie."

"Eh?" Tangor had no idea what his sister was talking about.

"It talks and it has wings, feathers, a beak – oh, and it headbangs mirrors, so that's the budgie bit. But it has flappy ears, hair, feety-hands and eats bananas, so that's the chimpanzee bit."

"Fantastic!" cheered Tangor. "So where did it come from?"

"Haven't you heard?" she said. "It's the latest craze, animal fusion. All the young gods are doing it. You just pick two animals, mix their deeyenay buds in a turbo evolver and see what you get."

"*Any* two animals?" gasped Tangor. "So what would you get with say, er … a porcupine and a hippo?"

"You'd get a poppo!" said Tangal. "It'd be huge and angry and covered in nasty spikes."

"Now that's really got my gravy boiling!" said Tangor excitedly. "Oh boy – I can't wait to see Urgum fighting a poppo. The barbarians are back in business!"

Just Like a Picnic

VATCHOOSH! Urgum wiped the green stuff off his sleeve and wished he'd found a better hiding place than in the shadow of the Sneezing Rock. Unfortunately, the Unsightly Hills of Nap didn't have much else to offer, and so Urgum stayed where he was, watching the large figure in a white dress wandering up and down the Dribbling Gorge. Every so often the figure paused to adjust its dress, which kept riding up over its large stomach, and check that the heavy stone club it was carrying was still safely tucked into the petticoat. Urgum grinned with excitement. The gorge was one of the main tracks through the hills, so it wouldn't be long before a few nappars came along. Urgum knew that the cowards wouldn't be able to resist attacking a lone

female. Boy, they were in for a surprise! Robbin might have been the quietest and politest of his sons, but he was also by far the best fighter. He'd have no trouble keeping a few nappars at bay until Urgum dashed down to finish them off. Divina and Molly were well away setting up their picnic somewhere, so as long as they didn't interfere, everything would be … well, just like a picnic.

High up in the sky were two black specks, the Golgarth vultures Djinta and Percy had arrived for a picnic too.

They often tracked

Urgum, knowing that he was likely to leave some tasty dead lunch behind him. They swooped and soared excitedly, which meant something was coming. Urgum ducked down behind the rock, clutched his axe and waited.

Down in the gorge, Robbin heard flappy footsteps lurching up behind him and reached for his club. Three irritating squeaky voices were jabbering away.

"She hasn't seen us."

"But we've seen the softhand girlie!"

"Fat softhand girlie!"

"Fat softhand girlie?"

"I've never seen a fat softhand girlie."

"And she hasn't seen us."

"But we've seen the softhand girlie!"

"Fat softhand girlie!"

"Fat softhand girlie?"

"I've never seen a fat softhand girlie …"

The nappars were suspicious and with good reason. Softhand women prided themselves on having legs like flamingos, but the dress had ridden up again to reveal what looked more like two fat hairy pig backs ending in two hulking sweaty feet. Robbin had hoped the nappars would come close enough so he could swing his club round and smash their knees off, but they'd stopped short. There was only one thing for it. He turned round, he looked up at them and he put on his prettiest smile. The nappars leered horribly, pulled out their dirty daggers and stepped forwards. Robbin stood up on to his tippy-toes, then with a dainty little skip, he whipped out his club and hurled himself at them.

WAMM CHACK BU-DACK

Urgum peered out from the Sneezing Rock to see Robbin land a few good shots before the nappars staggered back out of reach. Urgum was disappointed. Although he couldn't count them, he knew that nappars normally attacked in much bigger gangs than that. Surely there would be some more coming soon? Nappars were rubbish these days, only good for attacking softhands, so as Robbin was holding them off quite well, Urgum decided to hang on until some more arrived. It was hardly worth getting his axe dirty for that sad little bunch. But just then, a large figure on an ox came thundering down the path.

"LEAVE HER ALONE!" it screamed.

The nappars turned just as Mungoid caught up with

them. He slid off the back of his ox, and his massive fist immediately knocked one of the squitty faces inside out, and he booted another one halfway across the gorge. The ox itself was still charging, unable to stop or turn, and rammed the third nappar into a large boulder, which cracked down the middle. The dazed nappar slithered face down into a sticky pool of dribble. By the time Urgum had wandered over, Robbin had dragged all three into a messy pile and was jumping up and down on them with his white dress flying everywhere.

KA-JUNK KA-JUNK KA-JUNK

"Oi, Mungoid!" shouted Urgum. "What do you think you're doing? These are our nappars. If you want nappars, get your own!"

"What do you mean YOUR nappars?" demanded Mungoid. "I'm saving this very beautiful young lady."

"Why, thank you, Mungoid," said Robbin.

"She didn't need saving," said Urgum.

With a sick groan the nappars agreed.

"But she's a delicate little treasure," said Mungoid, watching in admiration as Robbin finished splattering them into the ground. "You had no right dragging her out here."

"She's Robbin, you clot!" said Urgum.

Robbin took one last leap high into the air and then brought his feet down on to the nappars with a mighty

KER-SPLOBBAH

"Well, how was I supposed to know it wasn't a lovely soft kind gentle little woman?" said Mungoid.

"You've spoilt my plan," sulked Urgum. "I was waiting for a load more nappars to turn up, but thanks to you there won't be any now."

"Sorry," said Mungoid sheepishly.

"Hardly worth taking this lot in," said Urgum. "We may as well leave them for the vultures."

"What vultures?" asked Mungoid, looking upwards.

Djinta and Percy were nowhere to be seen.

"That's funny," said Urgum. "They were here a moment ago."

"Look, Dad, they're over there," said Robbin, pointing over Urgum's shoulder. Sure enough, the two black specks were hovering in the sky over the next gorge.

"That's Tacky Valley," said Urgum. "It's where

Divina's set up the picnic! What are they doing there?"

Just then Molly's head appeared over the rocks. "Dad!" she shouted. "Mum says sorry to disturb you, but are you busy right now?"

"Very busy. Why?"

"She's surrounded by nappars."

Even as Molly spoke, the vultures were starting to swoop and soar again. Urgum and the others all scrambled over the clammy rocks and looked down into the valley. A tartan blanket was spread out on the ground and arranged on it were piles of giraffe ribs and pelican wings. Standing to one side of the blanket was Divina with her left eyebrow set to kill, while on the other side a gang of about twenty nappars was keeping well back. No wonder, Divina was holding out a teaspoon in a very threatening manner.

"The first one of you to put a foot on the blanket will regret it!" she warned them.

The nappars all gibbered away uneasily. They had never seen a teaspoon waved so scarily before.

"Robbin," hissed Urgum. "Get down there with Molly and back your mum up! Mungoid, see if you can send that lot back up the valley. I'll be waiting for them."

"OK!" said Mungoid.

"And take care, old friend," said Urgum. "It's dangerous down there."

"I'm not bothered by a few nappars," said Mungoid.

"Stuff the nappars," said Urgum. "Whatever you do, don't put your foot on the blanket."

"Why not?" asked Mungoid.

"Blankets are for sitting on, not feet," explained Molly.

"Yeah, so watch it," said Urgum. "Divina can get quite tetchy at picnics."

From high above, the two vultures wondered what dead thing would be left for them to eat. The whole gang of bandits with their ugly heads conveniently removed? That would have been their absolute dream first choice, but there were too many of them so that wasn't going to happen. Woman with spoon? Yes, she might die, especially as it looked like the gang had decided that twenty of them were brave enough to tackle her. But then a very meaty figure in a white dress had turned up. Ooh! That would have been tasty, but unfortunately the club it was holding meant that it didn't have plans to become dead yet. Pity. The little one? Well, no, that was Molly and the vultures quite liked her. It wouldn't be right somehow. As for the solid figure lumbering along with them, they knew from hard experience that under the skin, ungoids were mainly made of bone with a bit of granite thrown in, and they didn't die, they just crystallized. Yuk.

As Mungoid ran towards the nappars he let out a bone-quaking roar. What with that and the heavy boy in the white dress holding the club, not to mention the mad woman with the lethal teaspoon, the bandits had had enough. They turned and dashed away down the valley, much to the vultures' disappointment. Nothing dead, no dinner. But then suddenly – there was Urgum waiting at the end of the valley with his axe out. Good old Urgum! That's why the vultures always followed him. It was a very rare day when he let them down, and today wasn't one of them. They were going to get their absolute dream first choice of lunch after all.

YUM!

Tough, Mean and Don't Forget Filthy

After the picnic, Mungoid and Molly had gone home with the very empty wicker basket and the footprintless tartan blanket, while Urgum, Divina and Robbin went to collect the reward from the Laplace Palace Estate offices. Urgum had pushed his way straight in, but when Divina and Robbin tried to follow, the guards stopped them. One savage in the offices was already one too many for their liking. Divina wasn't too happy about being left outside in the street, but she didn't want to risk losing the money by making a fuss.

Urgum barged his way down the long corridor which lead to the bounty manager's office. Over his shoulder was a heavy sack bulging with large solid objects and behind him was a red line on the floor where blood had dripped from it as he'd walked along. In the distance were three softhands having a very important conversation about whose turn it was for the other two to write a poem about. Of course Urgum was only a savage, so they had no intention of moving out of his way until it suited them. Urgum knew this so he pulled one of the objects from the bag. It was about the size of a bowling ball and not too hairy, perfect for the job. He flung it down the passage at the softhands, who immediately climbed on to each other's shoulders to get out of the way. For a moment it worked, until they realized that none of them had actually got any feet on the ground, at which point they fell and landed in a screaming heap. Urgum gave the sack a little extra shake so it dripped a bit more as he stepped over them, just to remind them not to get in his way again.

When Urgum got to the door at the end of the corridor he kicked it open. The bounty manager looked up from behind her desk and immediately held her nose. She was a prim little woman wearing the green and gold robes of the Laplace Palace.

"I have come to claim the reward to prove that I'm

the toughest, meanest and filthiest savage in the Lost Desert," he announced proudly.

"Don't come in," she said.

"Why not?" demanded Urgum, who was already in.

"Because you stink," she said. "Don't you savages ever wash?"

A low growl came from the savage's lips. It wasn't a good idea to suggest washing to Urgum. He'd seen Divina washing and knew the dangers. You start with an innocent bit of water, but that leads to soap, then bubbles followed by sweet smells and the next thing you know you're gathering baskets of flowers while little birds tweet around your head, kittens rub up against your legs and butterflies land on your nose. Normally anybody who suggested washing to Urgum would be punished by utter death, but this woman was different. He knew that he had to prove to her that he deserved the reward. He swung the sack from his back and plonked it on the ground in front of him.

"This proves I'm the toughest," he said.

"We asked for dead or alive," said the woman looking at the sack dubiously. "Preferably dead, but if it's alive then hopefully it's well tied up and has been given a good thumping."

"I know that," said Urgum.

"So which is it?"

Urgum peered inside the sack. "Looks pretty dead to me," he said. "In fact they all do."

"All?" she said. "How many have you got in there?"

Divina had told Urgum the answer to this. He knew it was one of those number things, but he hadn't realized it mattered which one.

"Er … three-seventy-twelve," guessed Urgum.

"*How* many?" repeated the woman.

"I mean onety-eleven," said Urgum.

"Let's try again," she sighed and continued very slowly. "How – many – nappars – in – the – bag?"

"They're not complete nappars," explained Urgum. "There's a few bits missing."

"Missing? What's missing?"

"The bodies."

"Oh!" gasped the woman. "But they are dead, aren't they?"

Urgum looked into the sack again. "Yup. Still dead. Do you want to count them?"

Urgum swung the sack round and was about to tip it out on the floor.

"NO!" shouted the woman. She had gone as white as

a sun-bleached camel skull. "No, that won't be necessary! I just have to know what to pay you. It's a silver tanna each, so shall we say … fifteen tannas?"

"More," said Urgum. He didn't know anything about numbers, but he wanted to prove he was mean as well as tough.

"Then how about … thirteen?" said the woman. She hadn't meant to say a smaller number, but what with the smell and the blood dripping all over her floor, she hadn't been concentrating. She was about to correct herself when Urgum took her by surprise.

"That's better," he said, feeling rather pleased with himself. "But it's even more!"

"Ten?" By now the bounty manager had no idea what she was supposed to say to get this huge smelly savage out of her office, but if smaller numbers did the trick, that was fine by her.

"MORE!" Urgum was really enjoying being mean.

"OK, I'll say nine, but that's as far as I can go."

"Just a minute," said Urgum. He turned round and went into the corridor. He reached underneath the three softhands (who were frozen solid in shock) and pulled out the head he'd thrown, then marched back into the office and slammed it on the woman's desk.

"Don't forget this one," he said.

"All right, eight!" she quivered. "But that's it!" She unlocked a box on her desk and took out eight little coins and held them out towards Urgum, who grinned.

"Aha, the reward!" he said proudly as he took them. "That proves I'm the toughest and the meanest savage in the Lost Desert!"

He set off to the door, but just as he got there he turned back and checked the coins in his hand.

"This *is* eight, isn't it?"

The woman nodded, still trying not to breathe.

"Good, because do you know what happens to people who cheat me?" asked Urgum. The woman shook her head. Urgum picked up the sack and tipped all the twenty-three heads out. "That."

The woman managed not to faint. Urgum was about to leave again, but then a final thought crossed his mind. He pulled up his vest.

"Sorry, I forgot. I'm the toughest, the meanest *and* the filthiest. Look at my belly button."

And that's when she did faint.

While Divina and Robbin had been outside waiting for Urgum, a sedan sofa carried by six slaves had pulled up

alongside them.

"Divina *Dahling*!"
came a soupy voice.
Divina looked up and
saw one of her old
friends from her
softhand days
wrapped in a cloak
of peacock feathers,
and dripping with
perfume and jewels.

"Hello, Suprema,"
said Divina, self-
consciously checking
her hair. "You're
looking pampered."

"Thank you, dahling,
aren't I just?" said Suprema,
staring at Robbin. She continued in a whisper. "Oh, dahling, I'm so
sorry, I didn't know. Ugh! How awful for you."

"What?"

"Your daughter is just so ugly! Oh, if she'd been mine
I'd have fed her to crocodiles at birth. Obviously it's too

85

late now, but maybe you could lock an iron bucket over her head. Or how about face surgery? I hear they can do marvellous things with a large mallet these days."

"That is not my daughter!" said Divina. "That's my son, Robbin."

"How do you do, madam," said Robbin. He bowed slightly.

PING P-PING TOINK!

Some of the stitches down the back of the straining dress couldn't hold it any more, so Robbin quickly stood up again.

"Charmed, I'm sure," said Suprema, then to Divina: "It's worse than I thought! You haven't any money to give him proper clothes, have you?"

"We do have money actually!" snapped Divina. "My Urgum is in there right now picking up the reward money for capturing the nappar bandits. He's done ever so well, you'll see!"

And that's when Urgum came out with the smug grin on his face.

"What did you get, dear?" asked Divina. "Twenty?"

"More!"

"Thirty? Forty?"

"Ho ho!" laughed Urgum confidently. "More!"

"Fifty?"

"Well, whatever that is, you're not even close."

"How much then?"

"Eight!" said Urgum, proudly holding out the little coins.

Divina could have cried. Suprema was just *so* delighted that her face was almost caught unprepared. Her nose, mouth and cheek muscles had been preparing for this moment for years. All those long hours casually dismissing her servants, best labours, sniffing when her friends had smaller diamonds than she had, snooting when their clothes were half an hour out of fashion, this was the moment it had all been working up to. Every iota of her snobbish expertise was now brought into play as her nose and mouth locked together into the most devastatingly agonized superior sneer. It was a work of art.

"Dah-*LING*!" she screeched down her nose. "You don't have to live like this! I want to help you, after all we used to be friends. Obviously we can't be friends now, but I'm not a snob, so here's what I'll do. You can be one of my servants if you like! Well, technically you'll be a slave of course, but if you please me I won't have you whipped too hard and at least it'll get you out of … this!"

Urgum's brain was still trying to unravel what Suprema was saying, but his fist had already worked it out and had planned a rather clever answer. The six sedan slaves saw it and their eyes flickered excitedly, but then Divina saw it too and put her hand on Urgum's arm to restrain him.

"Robbin, my baby," she said. "I wonder if you'd be so good as to help me convey a message to my dear friend here."

"What's that, Mum?"

"Just be so kind as to turn your back towards her, please. Thank you. Now I wonder if you'd oblige us all by touching your toes? Thank you so much again." Just as Divina had planned, the stitching of the wedding dress couldn't take the extra strain.

FRAZZZUPP

The dress split apart right down the back and parts of Robbin that had never felt daylight before could feel it now. Once again Suprema's face was pushed to extremes as the mouth and eyes locked into the wide-open brain-has-been-disconnected-by-shock position.

"Well done, Robbin," said Divina. "I think that sums up everything I've got to say rather well."

Urgum put his fist away and smiled proudly at the

grinning slaves. "She's got a real knack for conversation has my wife," he said.

Riiiip!

The Turbo Evolver

Back in their cave, Urgum proudly laid the eight little coins on the table and shoved them towards Divina. "There!" he said. "That proves I'm the toughest, meanest and filthiest savage in the Lost Desert."

"You've done ever so well, Urgie," said Divina.

"Yeah, I know," said Urgum, who was an honest sort of chap. "So now you can go and treat yourself to something."

Divina smiled sadly. Eight silver tannas weren't going to be enough to buy something fabulously exclusive to fill the gap on her dressing table. But suppose she could talk him into doing it more often? Once again, the wifiest wife in the Lost Desert was scheming.

"You enjoyed getting the reward, didn't you?" she said

and Urgum nodded. "So you wouldn't mind doing it a few more times?"

"Ah! Well, I'm not sure about that..."

"Oh go on," she said. "Besides, it'd be a good excuse to go to the battle market for some new weapons."

The battle market! Urgum loved the battle market as much as Divina hated it. Usually her left eyebrow went into overdrive if he suggested a visit, but ever since she'd seen that reward thing in her *Modern Savage* magazine, she'd started to be a lot more reasonable. *Yippee!* thought Urgum. *Maybe this reward/money thing isn't so bad after all...*

Luckily the barbarian gods didn't know what Urgum was thinking, because up in the Halls of Sirrus they were busy with other things. The divine twins were staring at an odd looking box made from rock that was sitting in the middle of their table. A small window in the front kept flickering as ice and fire fought it out inside.

"Can't this evolver thing go any faster?" moaned Tangor.

"Evolution takes ages!" said Tangal. "It has to have time to eliminate the failures. We can't just chuck any two animals together and let Urgum fight the result without checking how they'll turn out. It's a good job we didn't let him loose on the poppo, all the other gods would have laughed at us!"

Tangor sighed and poked a tiny pink lump on the table with his finger. "It was supposed to have a huge hippo body covered in porcupine spikes!"

"Thanks to the evolver, we now know it has a little pink porcupine body, with no spikes, just two hippo teeth each the size of its head. You can't predict what you're going to get. That's the problem with evolution, but it's also part of the fun."

A phut of sulphuric smoke shot from the box.

"Aha!" said Tangal. "It's reached the Amnettoic era. It's about ready."

"The lion-woolly mammoth!" said Tangor excitedly. "Both animals, are big, fierce and with spiky bits. I can't see how this'll go wrong!"

Tangal opened the door to the evolver and looked inside. "Oh," she said. "It's very hairy."

"Hairy?"

"Very, very hairy," said Tangal, reaching inside. She pulled out a ball of fluff and put it on the table. It staggered about painfully, leaving a trail of white flakes behind it, then fell over and lay still.

"Oh dear, I think it's just died of dandruff," she said.

"I give in!" cursed Tangor. "The best thing was that chimp-budgie thing that Molly caught, but it was just too small."

"Maybe if we made a lot of them, we might get a really big one!"

"It's worth a try," admitted Tangor. "Although we might just get a whole range of revolting colours."

After several more turbo-speeded evolutionary cycles, it turned out that Tangor was right. Their table was covered in sickly blue, yellow, grey and primrose pink little budgie-chimps, all scratching their own armpits and asking each other "Who's a pretty boy then?" The two great gods peered down at them carefully.

"They're certainly nasty," said Tangal.

"If there was just one that was a bit bigger, he could be the leader," said Tangor.

"Maybe we could try a slight modification!" said Tangal. "We keep the budgie feathers and the beak …"

"… really horrible," agreed Tangor, nodding.

"…but instead of a chimp, why don't we try a gorilla?"

"A gorilla-budgie?" said Tangor. "What if it's the size of a budgie and just wants to pick its nose with its foot all day?"

"It's got to be worth a try," said Tangal. She had already picked out two tiny buds from a huge mixed jarful. She put them on a drop of nectar and carefully placed them in the evolver, then shut the door. Inside, the first tectonic collisions got under way.

Meanwhile, Tangor was thinking out loud. "Gorilla-budgie? The gorillabud?"

"The gorbudgie?" suggested Tangal.

"The gorgie?" said Tangor.

BLAMMM!

The door to the evolver burst open. Clouds of unformed elements and acid rains spewed out across the table, but striding unaffected through all of it was a chunky puke-green creature.

"Get it right!" it demanded. "I'm a GORGO!"

PART TWO:

THE BATTLE MARKET

The Night caller

It was the cold dead of night. Everyone and everything in Golgarth Cragg was asleep and a rich chorus of snorey noises was echoing out of the cave entrances dotted around the inside of the rock basin. The grunts of the seven savage sons neatly counterpointed the sharp snorettes from Divina, while beside her Urgum provided a wide selection of interesting sounds, some of which didn't come from his mouth. Over on the other side of the basin, Grizelda's melodic sighs were punctuated by the bat-like squeaks of her meebobs, but the best snorer was actually Mungoid. His heavily-boned head produced long sub-harmonic tones which soaked deep into the ground and travelled for thousands of miles, where they would finally cause dainty china ornaments to mysteriously fall off shelves in places that nobody had even heard of. The animals tucked away in the shadows of the cragg added to the mix, the ostriches purtooed, the ducks quuckered, the horses snuffaglopped and the rattlesnakes hifthssed. They all slept safe and sound thanks to the Giant Guardian of Golgarth.

Olk had been standing on guard at the entrance to the cragg for as long as anyone could remember. Olk was the guard that even other guards would never try to get past. This was partly because Olk was the massivest guard, and slung across his shoulder was the longest and foulest blade in the Lost Desert, but the main reason other guards didn't try to get past him was because they were too busy guarding their own places. It's what guards do, otherwise they wouldn't be guards.

Even the flies on Olk's blade were taking a rest and doing tiny little fly snores. They'd had a busy day flitting around the dark stains and smears along the jagged edge, but was Olk asleep too? Or was he awake? In fact he was both at once. He had a long scar down the middle of his head showing where a massive scythe had sliced his skull open years ago. His brain had been split into two bits, which was handy because the bits could take turns to be awake. While one bit was doing strange purply brain snores, the other bit peered out from one half-closed eye and passed the time by remembering Divina's complicated password, and making tiny balance corrections to stop the rest of Olk falling over.

Suddenly the awake half-brain detected activity. The on-duty ear had detected the smallest sound, a sort of whimpering chatter along with exhausted footsteps. The half-brain raised the eyelid and swivelled the open eye round to see a small solitary figure struggling along Smiley Alley towards the cragg, talking to itself. The half-brain cued the other half to wake up and together they switched the might of Olk into full operational mode.

From the outside, the long blade twitched just ever so slightly. BUZZ, went the flies. *What were we doing? Oh yes, flutting around being irritating. Oh lordy, we almost forgot.* Flit flit flit.

The small pathetic figure struggled up to Olk. He was shivering, hungry, and had walked halfway across the desert. Through the entrance to the cragg he could see flickers of fire, smell the remains of food. The big guard looked asleep, maybe he could just creep past unnoticed …

"PASSWORD." The noise rumbled out of Olk like a boulder falling down a well.

"Oh!" said the pathetic man, whose real name was Abill. "What password would you like? I know lots."

"THE password."

"Oh mercy, can we just do this tomorrow?" said Abill. "It's just that I seem to have lost my family and they do so worry about me, and they'd be much happier knowing that I was somewhere warm and safe instead of wandering the desert. I was trying to keep up with them but I could not because they had made me eat too much straw. That's how much they care about me, they were eating meat but because I was weak they said I should eat something better to build my strength up. If I wanted to be as strong as a horse I had to be like the horse and have a full belly of straw. So they kindly gave me straw and I tried to eat as much as I could but they forced more and more into me and finally, 'Hey, no more straw! Belly full,' I scream."

"WHAT?"

"'Hey, no more straw! Belly full,' I scream."

Olk's two half-brains discussed this. "Enormous strawberry fool ice cream?" It sounded like he'd said the password.

"ENTER."

Abill was surprised but grateful.

"Oh, thank you. Thank you. And I would gladly tell you the rest, but I am tired and must get a drink."

Olk's off-duty half-brain shut down and the blade stopped quivering, the flies landed on it and all was quiet again. Then a big SPLOSH came from the well outside Mungoid's cave.

An Early Start

Early the following morning the sun was just peeping over the rocks into Golgarth Cragg. Usually it wasn't worth the effort because there was nothing to peep at apart from the odd ostrich having a scratch, but today was different. For once, the seven sons were already up and by the time Urgum stumbled out of the cave rubbing his eyes and picking his ears, they were all mounted on their horses, fully armed and ready to ride.

"YARGHHH!" shouted the sons excitedly.

"Yawn," replied Urgum sleepily. "What's going on?"

"Oh, honestly, Dad!" sneered Ruinn. "Have you forgotten? It's the day of the battle market."

"WHAT?"

"Come on!" said Ruff. "We're all ready to go."

"But I haven't even had breakfast yet!" complained Urgum.

"THEN HURRY UP!" they all shouted.

With a happy skip, Urgum hurried back into the cave to get his belt and hat. Meanwhile in the kitchen, Molly and Divina were arguing.

"No!" said Divina. "And that's final."

"But Mum, WHY can't I go to the battle market?" pleaded Molly.

"Because all children must be accompanied by a responsible adult."

"But I'll be with Dad."

"He's NOT a responsible adult."

"Yes, he is," said Molly.

"No, he's not."

"YES, HE IS!"

At that moment Urgum threw himself into the kitchen, grabbed three fresh alligator livers out of a bucket and crammed them in his mouth.

"What ARE you doing?" barked Divina crossly.

"Habbling my bleckflast!" spluttered Urgum, causing bits of slippery purple meat to splatter everywhere. With both hands he hurriedly scooped up a puddle of curds from a bowl and sloshed them into his mouth while he was still chewing.

"Glub-bye!" he called, wiping his face on his hair and dashing out.

"Is that all you've got to say?" demanded Divina.

Urgum's head reappeared in the archway. For a moment he stood there with his jaw still frantically munching away, then he did a great gulping swallow, belted his chest with his fist and belched out an earth-quaking BURP. With a satisfied smile and a wave he was gone.

"See?" said Divina. "How can anyone with such awful manners be responsible. He's not even an adult."

"It's so unfair!" wailed Molly. "Why can't you take me then?"

"The battle market?" replied Divina. "Me? Oh no. All those ghastly little people trying to sell me their silly swords and bangpowder. I've got much better things to do."

"Then can I go with Mungoid?" asked Molly.

Divina hummed. "You can ask him, but he might be busy."

Molly stomped crossly out of the cave just in time to

see Urgum and her brothers charging out of the cragg and away down Smiley Alley.

"YARGHHH!" she heard them all cry together.

Never mind, thought Molly, Mungoid wouldn't let her down, but just then there was a massive ROAR from Mungoid's cave. She dashed over to see the great ungoid reach right down into his well and then pull out a skinny little man in a shabby purple robe. With one hand wrapped right around the man's neck Mungoid bellowed straight into his face.

"WHAT'S YOUR GAME, MATEY?" roared Mungoid. "And this better be GOOD."

"N-n-nothing!" said the small man helplessly.

"Talk!" said Mungoid, giving him a shake, making water fly off everywhere.

"Talk?" replied the little man surprised. "You want me to talk? Are you sure?"

"Of course I'm sure!" boomed Mungoid right in his face. "Tell me exactly who you are and what you're doing here."

"Oh golly!" said the little man. "If I talk, will you listen?"

"Yes, I'm listening!" snapped Mungoid. "Now talk."

"This is very strange for me," said the little man. "No

one has ever asked me to talk before and if I do talk people slap me or run away or tell me to shut up. Are you sure you want me to talk?"

"TALK OR I'LL BITE YOUR HEAD OFF."

To Molly, this sounded like excellent entertainment and highly suitable for girls, so she settled herself down on a rock to watch. The small man had been grinning uncertainly, thinking that Mungoid was joking, but the grin had quickly frozen on his face as he realized the massive ungoid jaw was slowly opening wider, then wider, then wider...

"He'll do it," said Molly helpfully. "Won't you, Mungoid?"

"Alla-ar-galla-garh," said Mungoid, who couldn't say much else because by now his jaws were far enough apart to go right over the small man's head. The small man tugged away helplessly at Mungoid's thick wrists and tried in vain to pull his head back from that great drooling tongue.

"Don't wriggle," advised Molly. "If he misses and just takes half your head off with the first bite, that can be really sore. If I were you, I'd start talking."

The small man stopped the struggle and went limp in Mungoid's grasp. Then clasping his hands together in prayer he began to talk. In fact, he began to talk a *lot*.

"Mercy, mercy, mercy!" he pleaded to start with. "My name is Abill and I have become separated from my family. We had been riding across the desert for days, or rather they had been riding and I had been running behind because my dear mother had accidentally pushed my horse off a cliff. I was very lucky to jump off in time, but after that I found it harder and harder to keep up, especially as my sister asked to borrow my shoes and then accidentally threw them away. But when I finally caught up with them they asked me to collect firewood, so off I went, but on my return I found they had already moved on and ever since I have been searching the desert for them..."

Still clutching the man's neck, Mungoid glanced over to Molly with mouth wide open and eyebrows raised.

"Mungoid, when you've finished with him, can I go to the battle market with you?" she asked. "Please?"

Mungoid released the small man, and with a creak and a slam, he closed his jaw up. The small man seemed to make no effort to escape, and Mungoid had already decided that, in any case, he'd make no effort to catch him.

"Yeah, come on, let's go," said Mungoid to Molly. "And thanks for your help. To be honest I hate biting heads off. It's just a party piece being able to get a head in your mouth, but once it's in, it's murder to actually chew through the neck."

"At least it got him talking," said Molly.

They looked back at the small man, who was still standing in the same spot looking at them wistfully. He cleared his throat and continued, "I still haven't fully explained why I was in your cave. As you insist on my giving the exact details, I must take you back to the day of my birth. My mother had already born forty-nine other children whose names were..."

Oh yes indeed, Mungoid had got him talking. And talking and talking and talking, and it didn't matter which way Mungoid turned his head, the little man simply stepped in front of him and continued talking.

Mungoid slumped to a rock, his shoulders sagged, his mouth fell open, no way was he going to get to the battle market that day!

Molly went off to find a nice place to sit and be miserable. "It's so unfair!" she moaned to herself.

"What is?"

The voice beside her made Molly jump. It was Grizelda the Grisly all dressed up in her finest leathers. Molly hadn't heard her approach, but then Grizelda had always been good at moving quietly.

"Hi, Grizelda," said Molly. "What are you all dressed up posh for?"

"I'm going to the battle market," said Grizelda. "I need to pick up a few, er ... bits and pieces."

"Arrows and knives and things?" asked Molly excitedly.

"Well, maybe," said Grizelda uncertainly. "It's fun to see what they've got. Aren't you going?"

"Mum says I can't," said Molly. "I have to go with a responsible adult, but Mungoid's busy and Dad doesn't count because he burps."

"That's tough luck," said Grizelda, as her two hairy meebobs ran up, leading her horse. "I'll see you later then."

But just as Grizelda leapt up on to her horse, Molly had an idea.

"Hey, Grizelda, do you burp?"

"I do not," snapped Grizelda without thinking.

In a flash Molly had climbed up on to the horse behind her.

"Then you can take me!" said Molly. "You're responsible."

"But, but..." complained Grizelda.

"Don't worry!" said Molly, hugging on to Grizelda's waist. "I've got some money and everything. The meebobs can tell Mum. She won't mind, she thinks you're dead classy."

Grizelda looked down at her two hairy meebobs in desperation and shrugged.

"Make sure you explain it exactly," said Grizelda.

"Snurt," said the meebobs, nodding their heads.

With a sigh, Grizelda turned her horse towards the cragg entrance, then spurred it forward. Molly hugged on even tighter as Grizelda's flame-red hair lashed around her cheeks. This was going to be her best day ever!

The Head of Security's Head

The battle market was held in the Laplace Hippodrome, the magnificent arena in the very centre of the Lost Desert. (Actually nobody was sure if the arena really was in the centre of the desert or not, because nobody knew where the edges of the desert were. But that's not important right now.)

The market was packed with stalls and

booths selling every weapon, accessory, outfit, gadget and dangerous spiky thing that a savage could possibly desire, as well as a few odd bits that nobody was remotely interested in.

"Yarghhh!" yelled Urgum and the seven sons as they galloped towards the market, dreaming of all the fabulous new gear they'd be bringing home.

"I want a new dagger," said Ruff.

"Pah!" scoffed Urgum.

"I'm having a new sword!" said Ruinn.

"Pah!" scoffed Urgum.

"I'm having a great big axe," said Rekk.

"I'm having an even bigger axe," said Rakk.

"Pah and pah again," scoffed Urgum.

"Dad?" asked Robbin. "Why do you keep scoffing pah?"

"Daggers, swords and axes…" sneered Urgum. "That's boring stuff. Boys, there's only one thing we're coming home with."

"What?" they chorused.

"We coming home with … *the most lethal weapon in the market*!"

"Wow!" replied the boys. "What's that?"

"Dunno yet," admitted Urgum. "But whatever it is, we're bringing it home, right?"

"RIGHT!" they all cheered.

"And I want a new dish mop," added Robbin. "I just hope they're not too expensive."

SKREEEECH!

Urgum heaved his horse to an abrupt halt.

WHUMP CLUNK THUDDA JOLT ...

all the other horses slammed into the back of Urgum's horse. Urgum turned to his largest son.

"What do you mean, *expensive*?" he demanded.

"We've only got eight silver tannas," said Robbin. "And

Mum's saving up for something for her dressing table, so we shouldn't spend it all."

The others all laughed mightily. "HO HO HO!"

"Robbin, we're BARBARIANS!" said Urgum, waving his axe. "We don't *spend*! The plan is that we charge in, we grab the most lethal weapon in the market – whatever it may be – and then we charge out. Spending's just for softhands!"

"But what if we get stopped?" asked Robbin.

"That's the clever bit!" boasted Urgum. "Who's going to stop us, when we've got the most lethal weapon in the market, whatever it may be?"

"Hurrah!" cheered the seven sons, and together they all spurred on their horses again.

"Will I have time to grab a pastry cutter too?" said Robbin, but Urgum pretended not to hear.

"Hey, Dad!" persisted Robbin. "I said I wanted a pastry cutter too."

"I'm pretending not to hear you," cursed Urgum, who wasn't very good at pretending anything. "Pastry cutter," he muttered under his breath. "The shame."

They rode up to the hippodrome and made their way to the horse park, which was already packed with thousands of horses of different sizes and colours all tied up.

"Can anybody see a gap?" asked Urgum, looking round desperately.

"There!" said Ruinn, pointing. But even as he stuck his finger out a tiny creature hopped into the gap, then took a *deeeeeeeeeeep* breath. It got bigger and bigger and bigger, until it was like a giant grey unnoticeable potato that was just neatly nudging the horses on either side. Then it put its feet in its mouth, curled up and went to sleep.

"Where?" asked Urgum. Ruinn looked again. Funny, there *had* been a gap, but it had disappeared. "We'll just have to leave the horses here, in the middle of nowhere," said Urgum.

Urgum and the sons got off their horses. Robbin put all the bits of Raymond into a large bag and hoisted him on to his shoulder. They were about to walk away when a little sweaty man in a blue uniform that was two sizes too big came hurrying towards them. He knocked the dust from his sleeves and straightened his big hat importantly. "What's going on?" he bellowed.

"Who's asking?" asked Urgum, drawing his axe.

"Oh, hello, Urgum," said the little man in a more friendly voice. "I might have guessed it was you."

"Hunjah the Headless!" gasped Urgum. "What are you

doing in a security uniform? You're the patheticest barbarian that ever lived."

"I'm head of horse park security," replied Hunjah proudly. "And you've got to tie your horses up to something."

Ruff laughed out loud. "Are YOU trying to tell US what to do?" he cried, then turned to his brothers. "Watch me, lads. I'll show you a head of security!"

Ruff raised his iron war mallet and prepared to smack it into the side of Hunjah's head.

"Don't do it!" said Urgum urgently.

"Why? I'm not scared of HIM." Ruff laughed and swung his mallet round mightily.

Hunjah's head flew through the air and landed in the sand still wearing the big blue hat.

"See?" said Ruff. "That's what I call a head of security. No body, just the head."

Ruff turned to his brothers expecting a round of applause and a bit of a cheer. Instead, they were staring in horror at the rest of Hunjah's body as it crawled its way across the sand, feeling for the head. At last the hands grabbed the ears and the head was swung back up on to the shoulders ... facing backwards. Hunjah rose to his feet to face them but his head was looking in the opposite direction.

"Where did they go?" he muttered to himself as dark blood slowly trickled from his neck.

"GULP!" gulped the brothers.

"I warned you," said Urgum. "They don't call him Hunjah the Headless for nothing."

Reaching his hands up to his head, Hunjah carefully

turned it around to face them. After a bit of squelching and a scraping of bone he was once again looking at Ruff.

"Ah, there you are," said Hunjah. "As I was saying, you have to tie your horses up to something."

Ruff didn't hear him as he was frozen solid in shock. The other sons came and poked their eldest brother.

"You all heard what the man said," said Ruinn. "I know what I'm going to tie my horse to."

A few minutes later Urgum and his six savage sons were heading into the hippodrome, leaving their horses tied to Ruff. Hunjah checked the ropes were tight. Very tight. He brought his face right up to Ruff's and smiled.

"Some days I love this job," he said.

Intelligent conversation

Back home, Divina was having an awkward time. The two meebobs had come to find her in the kitchen, where she was scraping some utterly delicious scrunchy old burnt bits of something off the fireplace. The meebobs were both covered in long hair and had huge hands and feet. The only other visible feature was their big eyes, which blinked at her desperately.

"Snurt," said one of the meebobs for the umpteenth time. He was pointing out of the doorway anxiously. "Snurt!"

"Snurt?" repeated Divina yet again.

"Snurt!" they both said together, nodding intently.

"Oh, you mean *snurt*!" said Divina.

"Snurt!" Both the meebobs hopped excitedly and nodded their heads.

In fact, Divina had seen Molly riding off with Grizelda, so she'd known all the time what they were trying to say even if she hadn't understood a single snurt. However, it was still a more intelligent conversation than she ever got from Urgum or the boys. She offered them each a bit of scrunch and tried a new word.

"Snurt?" she said, which seemed to do the trick.

Very delicately the two meebobs each helped themselves to a piece, but before eating it they did a little bow.

"Snurt," they said.

Divina realized that they had just said "thank you".

Intelligent conversation and then manners were so rare in Golgarth Cragg that a tear came to her eye. It reminded her of the slaves when she used to be a softhand. Always clean and polite, they had always been far nicer company than her so-called friends. She looked round the kitchen at all the logs that needed fetching, the dirty things that needed cleaning, the empty water tub... *Oh boy, wouldn't it be nice to have a slave again – and it might even be possible!* Although Urgum was useless at getting fabulously exquisite somethings for her dressing table, he was good at prisoners, so long as he remembered that they still had to be alive when he got them home. But would Urgum approve of her having a slave? She decided to ask the meebobs if they felt that Urgum would object on the grounds that it set a dangerous precedent particularly with regard to his personal stance towards softhand society within whose established traditions the privileged rich contemptuously exploited the masses of the downtrodden underclass.

"Snurt?"

"Snurt."

That was decided then. She'd tell Urgum to get her one.

Grizelda's Secret Shopping

When Molly and Grizelda arrived at the hippo-drome, Ruff had very kindly offered to let them tie their horse to him too. Well, to be precise, they had tied the horse up and he hadn't complained, or said anything, or even moved, so obviously he didn't mind. As Molly explained to Grizelda, not minding was the same as offering, which was very kind of him. Once they got inside they paused to adjust to the atmosphere. The whole market was packed with savages of all sizes, shapes and colours. Some were bargaining, some were arguing, some were starting fights, some were in the middle of fights and some had just finished a fight and were laughing or bleeding or cursing or starting their next fight. Some were just shouting "YARGHHH!" for no reason. It was fantastic.

Luckily, Grizelda seemed to know where she was going and, as she swept through the throng, like a miracle they all parted before her. A few sad bods tried to whistle or catch her eye, but they hadn't a chance. Molly felt so proud to be with her as she hurried along behind. There were so many brilliant things going on, Molly couldn't wait to see where Grizelda was taking her!

The stall selling spring-headed duelling mallets looked good, but Grizelda didn't even give it a glance. Maybe Grizelda was going to join the queue that was daring each other to jump over the pit of razor snakes? No, obviously that was too soft for Grizelda. Roast lizard twitching on a stick looked utterly yummy and smelt even better, but naff snacks were obviously not good enough for Grizelda either.

In the distance Molly saw a row of giant siege catapults. One of the machines suddenly lurched and a mighty cheer went up as a struggling rhinoceros flew high into the air. There was a scream of panic as the rhinoceros started to come down and everybody tried to run out of the way, then there was a huge laugh, as obviously somebody hadn't quite moved fast enough. Surely Grizelda was going to watch that! But no.

Grizelda pushed past cauldrons of smoky poisons, rows of shrunken heads, a very tall spike on which a mystic was balancing on his big toe...

"Grizelda!" said Molly, breathless with excitement. "Where are we going?"

At last Grizelda had stopped by a small lilac tent tucked in behind one of the giant catapults. She turned to Molly earnestly.

"Shhh!" she said. "Never mind all that silly stuff. This is the place we want. Girls' secret? Right?"

"Girls' secret!" agreed Molly proudly.

Molly couldn't wait to see what devastatingly nasty weapon Grizelda was going to get. Grizelda took a quick look around to check there was nobody she knew and then before Molly had realized it, Grizelda had whisked them both into the tent. A whiff of rich perfume shot up Molly's nose, making her blink.

"Aha! Good day, madam," beamed a very little old lady standing behind a large leather trunk. Next to her was a full-length mirror. She had a mountain of scarlet hair piled on top of her head and her long glittery earrings shimmered when she spoke. "Always such a pleasure to see you, Miss Grizelda."

"Have you got them in?" asked Grizelda hopefully.

"Just last week," said the little old lady, passing over a small carved ivory box. "I'm sure you'll approve."

With shaking hands Grizelda held the box to her face

and opened the lid. Molly held her breath in excitement. She couldn't quite see what was in the box but surely she could guess. It would probably be barbed spikes for Grizelda's arrows. Or maybe some phials of cobra venom. Or maybe some Attack Leeches that leap out of puddles and suck all your blood so fast that they explode. Molly couldn't wait to find out because whatever it was, Grizelda certainly looked pleased.

"Well?" said Grizelda. "What do you think, Molly?"

Out of the box, Grizelda pulled a pair of silky pink lace panties.

"It's so hard to find anything really nice to wear in this desert," said Grizelda, brushing them against her cheek. "Have a feel, Molly. It's fireworm silk, soft as a baby's breath."

Molly was so cross she could hardly speak, but already Grizelda had turned back to the old lady.

"You did mention a camisole top too?" Grizelda was asking.

The old lady raised her eyebrows and the lid of the trunk at the same time. She made some cooey noises and started to fumble inside, but Molly wasn't hanging around. In a fury she barged out of the booth to look for Urgum instead. He wouldn't be hard to find. For starters, there's no way that he'd be rubbing his pants in his face. Oh no, Molly knew exactly what her father would be doing. Urgum would be starting the biggest and bloodiest fight at the market.

First Encounter

At the same time over on the other side of the hip-podrome, Urgum was starting the biggest and bloodiest fight at the market.

Urgum had just left his axe at the grinders to have the blade sharpened, and he thought he'd see if he could get a fight in while he was waiting. There was a *thud thud thud* sound coming from a stall selling large mirrors for dazzling charging enemies, which seemed promising, especially as there was some sort of argument going on. The stallholder wasn't happy with a bunch of feather-covered savages who were banging their heads on the polished glasses and twittering, "Who's a pretty boy then?" They all looked like the bird thing that Molly had kept in the bear pit, all that is, apart from the pukey-green one. Urgum licked his lips in excitement. Although it also had a curved beak, handy-feet, grotty little wings and big flappy ears, it was twice as big as the others.

As Urgum wandered over, the smaller ones saw him and wisely moved away, but the big one wasn't bothered at all. Of course Urgum could have just walloped it, but that would have been a bit rude without a few introductory insults. What's more, if you can get the other savage to attack first, then even if it's only a weedy little prod, it puts the crowd on your side and they'll cheer as you bite, maul, mash and splatter your new enemy to bits. Urgum always enjoyed playing to the crowd, and by the time he was standing nose to beak with the feathered thing, a whole mass of people had hurried over to watch.

"Oi!" shouted Urgum. "Leave the man's mirrors alone or I'll have to give you a little spank on your bottom."

"Wooo!" went the crowd. What a nice cheeky dig! Surely the bird thing would fly at Urgum, swinging and ripping? But no, it just stared back. The fat black tongue flitted around its beak, the flappy ears twitched and picked up the excited whispers: "It's Urgum the Axeman!"

"So you're Urgum, are you?" came the reply. "I've

heard of you. I am Orgo the Gorgo."

"Orgo the Gorgo?" sneered Urgum. "Well, I've *never* heard of you."

"Wooo!" said the crowd again. What a beauty, and the gorgo had fallen right into it. Surely it would start swinging now?

"Your mistake then," said Orgo. "Because I happen to be the fiercest savage in the Lost Desert."

"Ou-ch!" giggled the crowd. Urgum hadn't liked that! Suddenly it was advantage to Orgo. Urgum was snarling and pointing an angry finger at him. Was Urgum about to dive in first? But no, the axeman swung his finger round and wiggled it in his ear.

"Sorry," said Urgum. "That sounded like *fiercest*. Surely you mean *funniest*, you green-feathered, headbanging, banana-chomping freak."

"Oh yo wowser!" went the crowd.

What a fantastic comeback, and it hadn't just offended the gorgo, it had also left him looking confused! He frowned and raised his left foot up over his shoulder to have a thoughtful scratch behind his ear. It didn't seem to help, so he shook his head and gave in. "All right," he said slightly crossly. "How do you know I like bananas?"

"Because my daughter had something like you for a PET," explained Urgum. "Until my mate Olk ATE IT."

"YAHOO!" went the crowd. Yet another dazzling verbal smash from the axeman. *Pet* and *ate it* was such a killer double insult, the gorgo had to fight now, he'd never find a remark to top that! The crowd held their breath as the tiny black eyes glared out from either side of the huge thick beak. Both hands and both feet were clenched in solid fists, the wings twitched with violent energy, but still he held back, and with good reason. Neither the crowd nor Urgum were ready for the brilliance of his answer.

"Oh, so you've got a daughter?" sneered Orgo. "A little girl … how *sweet*!"

The crowd didn't have time to "wooo" or "yahoo", instead they all dived backwards out of the way as Urgum reached for his axe and waved it over his head. Actually, the crowd needn't have worried because unfortunately for Urgum, he'd completely forgotten that he'd left his axe to be sharpened and all he was waving was a great big invisible nothing.

"Got a problem?" sneered Orgo. "I thought you were Urgum the Axeman?"

"I AM!" roared Urgum, staring at his empty hands in embarrassment.

"But you haven't got an axe," said Orgo. "All you've got is a daughter."

Urgum's eyes went red with rage. His voice dropped to the tone of a chill wind through a dead pelican's eye socket.

"When I said daughter, I meant sons!" warned Urgum. "Anyone'll tell you, Urgum and his seven savage sons are the scourge of the Lost Desert."

The crowd still kept back as the two savages stared at each other with fingers twitching. Hand-to-hand combat could be as ghastly as any other sort, especially if they started ripping whole chunks of flesh off each other. High overhead the vultures circled, and far, far higher overhead the two barbarian gods were looking down excitedly. Their plan was working perfectly. At last Urgum had a real enemy worth fighting, and what better place for it than the battle market? There was a huge audience all eager to see their barbarian champion do what he did best! This was exactly what Urgum needed, it was going to be a fight to the death and beyond...

...but just then a small person popped through the crowd and skipped up to Urgum.

"Hi, Dad!" said Molly.

"Who's that?" sniggered Orgo.

"Nobody," gulped Urgum. "I don't know."

"Dad!" yelled Molly. "Hello? It's me!"

Urgum turned his back to ignore Molly. Behind Orgo a couple of the mini-gorgos, one yellow and one grey, had pushed their way through the crowd and come to stand behind him.

"She called you Dad!" sniggered Orgo.

"No she didn't," said Urgum and then he turned round to shout at Molly, who was tugging the back of his shirt. "Can't you see I'm busy? Go away, Molly."

"MOLLY?" cried Orgo. "So you DO know who she is!"

"No I don't!" cursed Urgum. "She just keeps following

me round. GO AWAY, little girl! This is man's business."

"Great!" said Molly. "I like man's business. Just so long as you aren't wearing little pink silky pants."

"WHAT?"

"You aren't, are you?" asked Molly anxiously.

Orgo fell over, convulsed in laughter.

"Does she know something we don't know?" he bawled, slapping the ground.

By now all the other mini-gorgos were pointing and laughing at Urgum, and even the braver savages in the crowd were daring to smile.

"I'll take the lot of you bare handed!" screamed Urgum.

"What?" smirked Orgo. "On your own?"

"Get your eyes tested," challenged Molly, clenching her fists. "There's two of us."

A cheer went up from the gorgos, and some of them even clapped their hands and feet.

"We're impressed!" admitted Orgo.

Urgum looked down at Molly by his side. He was impressed too. There he was facing the gorgos, and out of all his offspring, who was the only one standing beside him? At a time like this, those boys should be with him. Where had they got to? But then a voice called out of the crowd behind Urgum.

"Dad! Get out of the way!"

Urgum turned round to see Ruinn grinning away next to the barrel of a cannon. The other boys were pushing it into position so that it was aimed directly at Orgo and all the mini-gorgos behind him.

"What's that?" gasped Urgum.

"The most lethal weapon in the market!" grinned Ruinn. "It's the Porta-Boom Mark 3, the lightest cannon ever made."

"We just, er … borrowed it," said Rekk.

"And we borrowed the very heaviest cannonball to go with it too," said Rakk.

Sure enough, a giant cannonball was rolling up beside the cannon, being pushed by the mysterious seventh son that everybody forgets about.

"But you don't know anything about cannons!" hissed Urgum.

"A bit of powder, nice big ball … whack 'em down the barrel and light it up!" said Ruinn. "So what's to know?"

For some reason, the gorgos hadn't bothered to move away, instead they looked on with amused interest.

"Haven't you forgotten something?" said Orgo.

"I've got the dish mop I wanted, if that's what you mean," shouted Robbin holding up a long stick with a bundle of cloth tied on the end.

"A dish mop?" wailed Urgum as he went bright red. "I can't believe a son of mine is waving a dish mop at Orgo the Gorgo."

Rekk and Rakk had opened a sack of black powder and were tipping it into the barrel of the cannon.

"Look out, Urgum!" jeered Orgo. "The powder's all over the place! Don't those boys of yours know to pack it all down to the bottom of the barrel? Otherwise the whole thing will just blow up in your ugly faces."

"He's bluffing," said Ruinn.

"No he's not!" snapped Urgum, going even brighter red. "You're supposed to have a stick with a pad on the end to shove the powder right down the barrel."

"Will this do?" asked Robbin, holding up his dish mop.

Urgum's eyes lit up as he grabbed the mop and turned to wave it at Orgo.

"Ha ha ha!" he laughed a triumphant laugh. "Look what I've got – a dish mop! Not laughing now, are you?"

"Too right," agreed Orgo. "You're too pitiful to laugh at. Now if you don't mind, we've got things to do." To Urgum's fury Orgo and the mini-gorgos wandered back to bang their heads on the mirrors and twitter "Who's a pretty boy then?" to themselves.

"Why do they do that, Dad?" whispered Molly.

"Something to do with their budgie brains," cursed Urgum, who was frantically plunging the dish mop into the cannon barrel to pack the powder tight. "But they won't be doing it for much longer because soon their budgie brains will be splashed all over the market. All right, boys, let's have that cannonball!"

With a heavy grunt, the boys hoisted the cannonball up and dropped it into the cannon, then heaved the whole thing round to aim it at the mirror stall. Finally they all stood back proudly.

"All right, you mirror-mad nutters," Molly shouted. "We're warning you, the cannon's loaded and ready to fire. This is your last chance to flutter your little wings and fly off."

"No thanks," said Orgo, giving his head another good bang on a mirror. "I'm busy."

Molly was astonished.

"What's going on?" she cried. "Have you any idea how stupid you look banging your heads on mirrors in front of a loaded cannon?"

"Trust me," replied Orgo, "we don't look as stupid as you! Haven't you forgotten something?"

Urgum turned on his sons in fury. "You spitwits! I know what he's thinking. You haven't got anything to light it with."

"Dead right!" The Gorgos laughed their awful laugh:

"Cakka Cakka Cakka."

"Dead wrong," said Robbin. He reached round and he pulled one of Raymond's bags from the sack on his back. Out from the bag popped a hand clutching a nice big fat match.

"Good old Raymond!" cheered the sons.

Robbin held the hand next to the fire hole of the cannon. Raymond struck the match on the barrel and it spat into life. Urgum looked over to the mirror stall and was glad to see that the smaller gorgos had stopped headbanging and were facing the cannon with their little wings twitching nervously.

"Not so funny now, eh?" boasted Urgum, waving his fist in a tough way. (Unfortunately it didn't look quite as tough as he imagined because he'd forgotten he was still holding the dish mop.) "You're going to regret calling me sweet!"

"Yeah yeah, whatever," said Orgo, then to Urgum's horror, he took a few steps *towards* the cannon. Staring straight down the barrel, Orgo reached up with his foot and gave himself a leisurely scratch under the chin with a long grey toe talon. "I still say you've forgotten something." As the match slowly burnt down in Raymond's hand, Urgum and the boys whispered urgently.

"Powder, ball, match … what else can there be?" asked Ruinn.

"Nothing," said Urgum. "He's bluffing!"

"We pinched everything off the stand," said Rakk.

"Except those wooden stakes," said Rekk.

"What wooden stakes?"

"You're supposed to bang them in the ground and fix the cannon to them," said Rekk. "If you can be bothered."

"And exactly what's the point of that?" asked Ruinn.

"Inertia."

"Eh?" they all gasped and looked round in amazement. They kept forgetting there was a seventh son, so when they heard the Other One's voice it always caught them by surprise.

"The mass of the iron projectile, i.e. the cannonball, is considerable in comparison to that of the portable cannon, and thus for maximum kinetic energy transfer following the combustion of the powder, the lighter of the two objects, i.e. the cannon, must be secured so as to ensure that the other gains the benefit of thrust from the reaction..."

... but Raymond was still holding the burning match and at that moment the flame caught his fingers and he dropped it on to the fire hole of the cannon.

What the seventh son had been trying to say was that unless a cannon is far heavier than the cannonball, it must be fixed to the ground otherwise

it'll move backwards.

KABABBA-BOO

M!

So if the cannon is far *lighter* than the cannonball...

... well, as it turned out, the Porta-Boom Mark 3 shot itself backwards and embedded itself in the hippodrome wall, taking all the sons with it. As for the giant cannon-ball, it stayed exactly where it was. For a split second

Urgum stood there staring at it stupidly as it hovered in mid-air, but once the cannonball had realized the cannon had gone from around it, it fell to the ground with a soft

PLUMCH,

smashing several bones in Urgum's foot.

"Congratulations," hooted Orgo. "You really have found the most lethal weapon in the market. It's splattered all your sons against the wall and smashed your foot."

"*Cakka cakka cakka* ..." the foul laugh of the gorgos echoed right across the hippodrome.

"That does it, bird-breath," muttered Urgum through gritted teeth as he yanked his flattened foot out from underneath the cannonball. "We're going to get something even more lethal and come for the LOT of you." Trying to look as dignified as possible Urgum turned his back and limped away, still holding the dish mop.

"Come on, Molly," he said, waving her to join him.

"I'm sorry," said Molly blankly. "Have we met? Do I know you? I don't think so."

And with that she dashed off in the opposite direction.

The Amber Mamba

Molly wandered around the battle market having the worst day of her life. It should have been so brilliant, but Grizelda had let her down, her family had been laughed at and all she had to spend was three bronze tannas. She had been looking forward so much to buying something, but even the naffest little wooden daggers had been ten bronze tannas and they weren't sharp enough to cut an old banana. Once again she walked past the giant siege catapults. Wow – wouldn't she just LOVE to have one of those? As she walked along watching a horse and cart being launched over the hippodrome wall, she stumbled over an old wicker basket lying at the side of the path.

"Watch it!" said a boy sitting cross-legged on the floor beside it.

"Sorry," said Molly. "Stupid place to leave a basket anyway."

Molly bent to put the basket back where it was, but the boy quickly shouted, "NO! Leave it."

Molly pulled back in surprise as the basket started rocking and thrashing around by itself. Quickly, the boy pulled out a small reed song pipe and played a very fast melody. A long orange snake suddenly shot from a hole in the basket, and started flicking itself around on the ground. It was an amber mamba, one of the meanest snakes in the desert, and on seeing Molly, it threw itself at her left leg and wrapped itself right around like a long bandage. Molly stood absolutely still. She knew that the slightest move would cause it to strike with enough venom to flatten an elephant.

Soon the mamba's head started to sway in time with the boy's music, and before long it had uncoiled itself and slid to the ground. To Molly's amazement the snake reared up in front of the boy and then began to do the most fabulous snake dance.

"That is awesome!" Molly whispered.

The boy smiled and then, pausing for the briefest of breaths, he said: "Watch this!"

He pulled a small metal hoop from his pocket and tossed it over the mamba's head. The mamba flexed from side to side and the hoop span round and round its body without sliding down. With a final flourish of music the boy stopped and the mamba flopped to the ground and fell to sleep.

"You did well to stand so still," said the boy.

"I didn't want to be dead!" grinned Molly.

Molly soon found that the boy was having as bad a day as she was. He was called Malzam, and he'd been performing with the amber mamba since sunrise, but so far not one single person had dropped a coin in the little wooden cup at his feet.

"I hate the battle market," said Malzam. "No one's come to see me."

"So why are you here?" asked Molly.

"I have to help my dad get the big catapults set up," said Malzam. "He demonstrates them. Spends all his time throwing big stuff in the air. Gets a bit boring after a while."

"How can it be boring?"

"Oh, believe me," said Malzam. "When you've seen one flying giraffe, you've seen them all. Still, better get back to work."

So saying, Malzam started playing again and the mamba got up and danced. Molly watched for a while then took her three bronze tannas from her purse and dropped them into Malzam's cup. Malzam was so surprised that he stopped playing. For a moment the mamba looked around uncertainly.

"You don't have to do that," he said.

"I do," said Molly. "I think that's the best thing I've seen for ages."

"I owe you a big favour, Molly!" called Malzam. "Anything, just ask."

Molly waved and turned to go. Malzam waved back and even the mamba waved its tail.

I've made friends with an amber mamba, thought Molly to herself. *That's got to be worth three bronze tannas.*

The Miracle
Mini-club

Urgum had been wandering round desperately look-ing for what was *really* the most lethal weapon in the market, so he could get his own back on those revolting gorgos. As he passed a small tent, he heard two of his favourite noises.

CRUNCH!

"OOYAH!"

If Urgum could have read the sign on the tent he
would know it said *The Miracle Mini-Club*. He peered
inside and saw a very large man on his knees clutching

his head in his hands. All he seemed to be wearing was a pair of leopard-skin trousers, and the muscles along his shoulders and arms looked like a row of brown melons. This was one extremely powerful savage, and yet his eyes were watering, his teeth were clenched and he was gently rubbing the top of his head. Standing over him was a little fellow with a big moustache who was looking very anxious.

"You OK?" asked the little fellow.

"Just about," groaned the large man as he tried to stagger to his feet. "You've got to be careful with that thing."

Urgum stared at what the little fellow was holding in his hand. It was a black shiny piece of wood about the size of a big thumb. "What's that?" he asked excitedly.

"You don't want to know," cursed the large man. "They should be banned."

"Sounds like my kind of weapon!" grinned Urgum.

"It's the Marvellous Miracle Mini-Club," said the little fellow. "It's a lot smaller than a normal club but a whole lot more powerful."

"Ooh!" said Urgum, sounding impressed. On the ground behind the little man was a whole box full of mini-clubs.

"You've enough there to tool up an army," remarked

Urgum. "But do they really work?"

"Of course," said the little man. "If you want a test, let me give you a soft tap on the head."

"Don't let him!" said the large man. "He almost smashed my skull in."

But Urgum didn't want to look soft, and besides he was most interested. He took off his hat and bowed his head all ready for a good solid whack.

"Wait!" said the large man. "Let me out of here first, I don't want any more of this."

Urgum and the little fellow chuckled as the large man staggered out of the tent clutching his head. When they were alone the little fellow raised his arm.

"How hard do you want it?" he asked. "Pick a number between one and five. One is the softest, five is the hardest."

"Thirteen," said Urgum, thinking that would be somewhere in the middle.

The little fellow gulped.

"Are you sure?" he said.

"Get on with it," said Urgum. He took a deep breath and clenched his eyes tight shut. If he was going to be hit *really* hard he didn't want his eyeballs popping out.

In front of him, Urgum was aware that the little

fellow was raising his arm ready to strike him with the club. What he didn't know was that immediately behind him a small panel had opened in the tent flap. The large man was looking through from the other side and, judging by the grin on his face, he seemed to have completely recovered. Winking at his small companion, the large man pushed a massive rock club through the hole in the tent and, holding it with his outstretched arm, he raised it above the back of Urgum's head.

"Ready?" the little fellow asked Urgum.

"Go for it!" said Urgum. The muscles on the large man's arm bulged and the club smashed down on to the back of Urgum's head.

KARRUNCHHHH

Of course, by the time Urgum had recovered consciousness, the panel in the tent had been closed and the large man had disappeared. Urgum sat up and saw two identical small men with big moustaches in front of him. Gingerly he reached round to feel the back of his head and felt a warm mass of bloody hair covering an impressive bump. Gradually the two small men merged together into one person with one moustache who was staring at him anxiously.

"Are you with us again?" said the little fellow. "That's good. Now be honest, what do you think? I could have hit you a lot harder, but I don't want to kill my customers until I've got their money, do I?"

Money! Urgum had forgotten about that.

"How much?" asked Urgum.

The little man took a deep breath. He knew he had to sound confident, which wasn't easy when he was standing in front of the fiercest savage in the Lost Desert who'd just been smashed over the head by his assistant. How much did he dare ask for?

"Thirty-six silver tannas each," said the little man. "You know they're worth it."

"Absolutely," said Urgum. With his head still swimming, Urgum stepped out of the tent just in time to see the boys passing.

"Hey boys!" said Urgum. "What do you think of this?"

The sons gathered round and admired Urgum's wound.

"That came from the most lethal weapon on the market," said Urgum. "It's the Miracle Mini-Club and there's a whole box of them in there. The only problem is we have to pay for them."

"PAY?" they all gasped in shock. "But we're barbarians!"

"But we're not *stupid* barbarians," said Urgum. "If we all charge in there and try to pinch them, he just needs to throw the box at us and we'll all be pulped to porridge. Anyway, they only cost sixty-thirty number thingies each. Who's got the money?"

"Me," said Robbin. He held out the coins, which looked tiny in his huge hand. "But we've only got seven tannas left, plus one dish mop."

"Seven's just fine," said Urgum taking them. "Any money left over can go to your mum's dressing table."

"Are you sure these clubs are worth it?" asked Ruinn.

"Of course," said Urgum. "If you don't believe me

you can always come in and have your skull cracked open." So they all decided to believe him and Urgum went back into the tent to see the little man. "I'll take the lot," said Urgum, pointing at the box of clubs.

"Really?" gasped the little man. Urgum smiled and nodded. "*Really?* Then I'll, er ... just work out what it all comes to." He couldn't believe his luck as he started to multiply thirty-six by another big number which he hadn't chosen yet.

"Don't you worry," said Urgum. "I'm good at sums. Sixty-thirty thingies for each one means the whole box costs exactly ..." he slammed the seven coins into the startled man's hand, "... that much."

"Um, er, ooo, ah, well, that's not exactly what I make it..." said the little man doubtfully.

"Oh really?" scowled Urgum.

The little man panicked as it dawned on him this was an extremely nasty savage with a bleeding head. Had he realized he was being tricked? Suddenly the savage reached out for him ... eek!

"Actually you're right," said Urgum. He took one of the coins back. "These two are for my wife's dressing table."

Moments later the little man was alone in his tent. It

could have been a lot worse, and he knew it *should* have been a lot worse. He grinned and no wonder. He was alive and he'd just sold a box of cupboard door knobs for six silver tannas.

The Wrong Tent

A steady *thud thud thud* noise was coming from a stand called Highly Polished Silver Shields along with merry little chirps of "Who's a pretty boy then?" Urgum and the sons were hiding around a far corner, each holding a mini-club and looking at it doubtfully.

"So do they really work?" asked Rekk.

"We'll soon see!" said Rakk, raising his club over Rekk's head.

"NO!" ordered Urgum. "Save it for Orgo and his feathered friends!"

The boys still looked unsure, so Urgum started up their battle chant.

"ARE WE SCARED?

NO!

Do we CARE?

NO!

We're completely

MENTAL!"

"Then CHARGE!"

screamed Urgum.

"YARGHHHH!"

The first the gorgos saw of Urgum and the sons was in the reflection from the highly polished shields. As the shields weren't flat, it made things seem rather oddly sized and shaped. In particular the clubs looked HUGE.

"ARGHHH!"

screamed the gorgos, who hadn't had time to turn round before Urgum and the sons were upon them. A mighty barrage of blows rained down from the mini-clubs.

Pink dink tinky-donk...

"Take that!" shouted Urgum, who had singled out the big green gorgo for himself, and brought his mini-club smashing down on to Orgo's head with all his might. It bounced off with a quiet *bink*.

"YOW!" screamed Orgo, clutching his head. But when he realized he hadn't actually felt anything he said: "Eh?"

"Don't pretend it doesn't hurt," said Urgum.

"Who's pretending?" asked Orgo, turning round and seeing the mini-club properly for the first time.

Urgum was getting worried. Either Orgo was a lot tougher than he'd realized or...

"Hey!" he shouted to the gorgos. "Are any of you getting hurt at all?"

"Not really," they replied, turning round. "Who's a happy boy then? Who's a happy boy?"

"See?" said Orgo. "No blood or bruises or bits chopped off or anything."

"Ow!" said the grey gorgo who was being hit by Robbin. "My eye stings a bit."

"Aha!" said Urgum. "At least Robbin's mini-club works."

"I haven't been using my mini-club," said Robbin. "I was hitting him with my dish mop." Robbin slapped his dish mop into his opponent's face again.

"Ow!" yelped his victim, covering his face with his hands and stumbling backwards into his mates. "Look out, he's got a dish mop!"

"Eeek!" said the gorgos, backing away.

"I've got a pastry cutter too," said Robbin.

"That does it," said Orgo. "If you want to play nasty, then you've asked for it. ATTACK!"

From under their wings the gorgos pulled out long curved cutlasses.

"YARGGHHH!" said Urgum, pulling his savagest face and raising his mini-club. "Come on, boys, we can still take them."

"Who's this 'we' you're talking to?" asked Orgo.

Urgum looked around to see the

boys running off into the distance. Even Urgum didn't fancy facing a pack of gorgos with cutlasses when he was alone and only armed with a little fat stick.

"Come back, cowards!" he ordered, running after his sons.

All the gorgos chased after them except for Orgo, who couldn't move for laughing. Urgum and the sons charged down passageways and through side alleys, then suddenly in front of them they spotted a small lilac tent.

"Quick, hide in here!" said Urgum.

They all dived in through the tent doorway.

SHREEEEEK!

They all dived back out again and threw themselves on to the ground as a hail of arrows shot out over their heads. The gorgos that had been running after them didn't have time to duck.

"Urgh!"

"Argh!"

"Ooof!"

Three gorgos were got by arrows, the others stopped

in their tracks.

"Ha ha, you fell right into our trap!" laughed Urgum from the ground.

"What trap?" asked Robbin, who was lying next to him.

"Shut up," hissed Urgum.

The gorgos turned and headed away, but as they did so the grey one turned and shouted: "Orgo isn't going to like this! Whoever's in that tent is going to be very sorry."

"Who *is* in that tent?" wondered Urgum aloud.

Just then the little old lady with the scarlet hair stuck her head out crossly.

"Miss Grizelda is in the tent!" she snapped. "And if you don't mind, Miss Grizelda does not like to be disturbed when she is changing."

Urgum blushed furiously as the little old lady put her head back inside.

"Dad?"

"Oh no," muttered Urgum as Molly came round the corner. "This is all I need."

"Did I see that?" asked Molly. "Did I really see that?"

"See what?" asked Urgum innocently.

"Urgum the Axeman, and his savage sons were being

165

chased by a bunch of budgie-brains into a ladies' underwear booth?"

"It wasn't like that," said Urgum.

"So what was it like?" demanded Molly. "I've NEVER been so ashamed. If you had any pride at all, you'd get out of here before you make an even bigger fool of yourself. Everyone's laughing at you."

"They wouldn't dare!" cursed Urgum.

But they would dare and they did dare. An amused crowd had gathered to see the sons all lying in the doorway of the underwear booth clutching their mini-clubs. Slowly and painfully the boys pulled themselves to their feet.

"That does it," said Urgum quietly. "I've had enough of today. We're going home."

As they set off towards the exit, Molly stuck her head inside the booth. Grizelda was slinging her bow across her back as the little old lady was wrapping up a parcel for her.

"Grizelda, you better get out of here!" said Molly. "You've just shot three little gorgos and they aren't happy. They said they're coming back."

"Gorgos?" asked Grizelda.

"Nasty beasts," said the lady. "But they do make good fans."

The old lady reached into her trunk and pulled out a large fan of brightly coloured gorgo feathers.

"Oh wow!" said Molly. "If they see that they'll go berserk. You'd better get away too."

"Yes," agreed the old lady. "It's probably better that they don't find either of us."

Immediately she slammed the trunk lid down and Grizelda helped her wheel it out of the booth. Together they disappeared down to the far end of the market, leaving Molly alone in the lilac tent. The only thing left behind was the large full-length mirror. Molly sighed. It really had been a rotten day. Everything had gone wrong. Maybe she should have been a gorgo, at least they seemed to have fun. She went up and stood next to the mirror.

Why not? she thought.

Thud thud thud.

"Who's a pretty girl then?" she said while banging her

head. "Who's a pretty girl then? Who's a ... *clever girl then?*"

Suddenly Molly dashed out of the tent. Could she find Malzam again in time? She ran full speed round the corner towards the giant catapults, and yes, there he was, still playing on his pipe. There were still only three bronze tannas in his cup, but when he saw Molly he grinned.

"Malzam!" gasped Molly. "You know that favour you mentioned...?"

What Goes Up...

"GWARK GWARK." The gorgo cry could be heard right across the market. Orgo was gathering every gorgo in the place to join him. Somebody had used three of the gorgos for target practice and so he was going to make sure that somebody would suffer a lot. Before long his multicoloured gang were assembled, all with their curved cutlasses drawn and ready. It was a ghastly sight and everyone else stepped well aside as the gorgos marched towards the little lilac tent.

"Come out, whoever you are!" cried Orgo into the doorway. "We've got business to settle."

To his surprise, Molly stepped out.

"Oh, hello, Mr Orgo," she said. "Have you come to buy some little pink pants? If so, I'm afraid you're a bit late."

"YOU!" gasped Orgo. "What are you doing in there?"

"If you must know," said Molly. "I've been preparing the most lethal weapon in the market."

"Oh have you?" snorted Orgo. "We'll soon see about that! Get out of our way little girl."

Orgo pushed Molly aside, then summoned all the other gorgos to follow him.

"Ready?" he yelled. "CHARGE!"

And with a terrible screeching war cry, all the gorgos dived inside the tent. Then it all went rather quiet. Very cautiously the people standing nearby approached to hear what was going on.

"Who's a pretty boy?" came the twittering voices along with the *thud thud thud* sounds of heads banging on a mirror. "Who's a pretty boy then?"

"So far so good!" muttered Molly to herself.

Taking a long piece of rope, she quickly crawled round the outside of the tent, threading it through all the peg holes. At the same time, the arm of a giant siege catapult was being slowly lowered into position overhead, and sitting on it was Malzam. Molly quickly gathered up the loose ends of the rope and tossed them up for him to catch. Malzam lashed the rope on to the very end of the massive arm, then once it was secure he crawled down to the centre of the catapult and hopped to the ground.

"All set, Dad!" he announced to the huge jolly man who was adjusting the ratchet controls of the catapult. Molly carefully approached the tent door and listened.

Thud thud thud.

All seemed ready, so Molly stuck her thumb up towards Malzam's dad. The large man grinned a big version of Malzam's grin and prepared to let the main ratchet slip a couple of notches. Just as he was doing so, Orgo stuck his head out of the doorway and came face to face with Molly.

"There's no weapon in here!" he scowled at Molly. "There's just a rather nice big shiny ... *eek!*"

With a great creak the arm of the catapult jolted upwards slightly. It was enough to draw the rope around the base of the tent tight and then hoist it into the air, tipping the entire tent upside down. Only one small cord was left connecting the tent to a final peg in the ground. Molly was still face to face with Orgo, but Orgo's face was now upside down and it was also very, very cross. From behind him inside the tent came a selection of screeches, thuds and curses.

"Oi!" screeched Orgo. "You let us go!"

"Not yet," said Molly. "First you say sorry for calling my dad sweet."

"Never!" cursed Orgo. "Now you let us go right now or you'll be sorry."

"Oh, all right then," said Molly. "If you really want me to let you go, I'll just let you go then. You asked for it."

And with that, Molly reached for the final tent peg and started tugging at it.

"NO!" screeched Orgo, suddenly realizing what he'd said. "Don't let us go..."

BAY-OY-iNGGG!

The peg came out and the giant arm of the catapult swung skywards, taking the tent with it. When the arm clanked into the upright position, the rope slipped free and the whole screeching, bulging bag of gorgos flew high and away right over the hippodrome wall, leaving a trail of coloured feathers gently fluttering to the ground behind it.

The crowd roared in delight, and no one was happier than Malzam's dad.

"Thanks for your help!" said Molly.

"Thank *you*!" he said. "That's the best thing I ever launched."

... Must Come Down

Nobody ever liked Ruff much, but on the trip home he was especially unbearable. They'd taken their horses, leaving him tied up to Grizelda's, but he'd wriggled free and was riding along beside them. He'd heard what had happened from all the other savages that had been leaving the market, it had been the best gossip of the day.

"You great bunch of Bettys!" Ruff was saying. "You'd never catch *me* blasting myself backwards into a wall with a cannon."

"Shut up," they all muttered.

"And you'd never catch *me* trying to attack a pack of gorgos with a few little fat sticks."

"Shut up shut up," they all muttered.

"And you'd never catch *me* being chased into a ... what was it again? Oh yes, I remember ... a ladies' pants shop!"

"Shut up shut up shut up!"

"The gorgos must be laughing silly at you all!" sneered Ruff. "But at least they can't laugh at me because you'd never catch *me* blasting myself backwards into a wall with a cannon..."

Just then Urgum spotted something curious.

"Hey!" he said. "Isn't that our vultures Djinta and Percy? Looks like they've found something tasty."

"What is it?" asked Robbin.

They all rode across to see what the vultures were circling over. It looked like a very large lilac bag tied up with rope and dripping with blood. From inside came a sad assortment of groans and whimpers. Urgum jumped down from his horse and sliced the bag open with his axe. A mass of brightly coloured feathers and broken mirror glass fell out.

Just then they heard a horse galloping up from behind them. It was Grizelda with Molly clinging on behind her.

"So that's where it landed!" said Molly as the horse reared to a halt. "I wondered how far it would go."

From the hole in the bag, a pale green head stuck out.

It didn't look well.

"Hah!" shouted Urgum. "I think that proves who's the fiercest savage in the desert!"

"You're right!" muttered Orgo. "But it's not you."

"Oh, come on!" said Urgum. "It isn't you!"

"No, it's not me and it's not you."

Urgum and the boys looked at each other blankly. Orgo raised a weary finger and pointed it at Molly.

"It's HER!"

PART THREE:

THE SAVVY AWARDS

The Big Sulk

For several days Urgum had been sitting high up on the ledge above the entrance to the cragg, muttering, polishing his axe and staring out towards the Wandering Jungle. He didn't eat and he didn't sleep, because he was far too busy letting his brain drown in a gluey blue ocean of SULK. The first few days of sulking had been fun because Molly and the others had kept coming up and asking, "Are you all right?" and he'd been able to shout back, "Leave me alone." Unfortunately, they'd eventually decided that they *would* leave him alone, and that had make him sulk even more.

Orgo had been right. It wasn't Urgum and the boys that had beaten the gorgos at the battle market, it was Molly. It was *so* unfair! Urgum was supposed to be the fiercest savage in the Lost Desert, not his ten-year-old daughter. But he'd show them, he'd show them ALL. Ever since he'd got back from the battle market Divina had been nagging him to get her a slave, so he was going to give her one – Orgo! Yes, once he'd caught that feathered freak and made him into a tame, timid little slave, that would prove to everyone who was the fiercest savage in the Lost Desert. It wasn't the nappars, it wasn't the oversized budgies, it wasn't anybody or anything else, it was URGUM. He stared out towards the Wandering Jungle, polished his axe and waited for a little *ding-a-ling*.

The little *ding-a-ling* was going to come from a bell that was tied to a string that was tied to a thin cloth that covered a deep hole that was full of sloppy tar that was next to Divina's big lovely shiny MIRROR that was in the middle of the Wandering Jungle. Brilliant!

Urgum tried his hardest to congratulate himself on inventing the Gorgo trap, but he wasn't helped by the others who claimed that Molly had actually invented it first when she'd caught the small blue gorgo thing. Molly! Hah! What did she know? Yes, all right, she'd also suggested putting the mirror up, and yes, she'd thought of the bell, BUT ... it was Urgum who had very cleverly built the trap the day before the Wandering Jungle had its banana season. Overnight every tree and shrub and even some animals had suddenly sprouted huge thick yummy bananas, and the gorgos would never be able to resist that! The fact that Urgum hadn't any idea there was going to be a banana season had nothing to do with it. As far as he was concerned it was a bit of pure brilliance even if the others said it was pure luck.

Actually it wasn't pure brilliance *or* pure luck. The barbarian gods had been keeping a careful watch on Urgum and were delighted that their ridiculous experiment in animal fusion had given him something to hate so much. Ever since the battle market, Urgum had been far too busy sulking to give any thought to money, and besides, a big sulk was always good for barbarians because it pointed them in the right direction. Urgum's head was stewing with marvellously murderous thoughts, setting him up for the most glorious and gruesome fight, so all the gods had to do was make sure he got one. That's why they had decided to help him catch the gorgos.

On the night after Urgum set the trap up, two bees materialized on Divina's mirror frame, the pollen baskets on their hind legs packed with turbo-speed banana deeyenay.

"Right," said Tangor, peering round the dark jungle. "This stuff's absolutely knock-out strength, so where do we put it?"

"On the ends of branches," said Tangal. "And try to be neat. We don't want to upset the jungle or it'll just wander off."

BUZZZZZZ

Tangal flapped her tiny wings and rose into the air, but then wobbled, flipped over, zizzed along upside down and accidentally pollinated a row of swamp tulips. Immediately their heads got longer and yellower and generally bananarier.

"Honestly!" grumbled Tangor. "Watch me and learn."

BUZZZZZZ

Tangor shot up into the air, looped the loop, and then landed with a bump, very nearly stinging his own bottom.

"Learn what?" laughed Tangal. "How to crash?"

"Phew, you've got to admire bees," admitted

Tangor. "How do they steer? Anyway, I might as well pollinate this old log I've landed on."

"Log?" said Tangal. "It's got teeth in one end!"

"Oopsy!" sniggered Tangor. The confused crocodile crawled away with bunches of bananas already swelling and ripening on its back.

It was no good. Bee flying with loaded leg baskets was never going to be easy, so in the dark they just blundered about dumping their banana deeyenay all over the place, pollinating everything in sight and giggling their abdomens off. Finally they dematerialized back up to the Halls of Sirrus to find they'd splashed so much deeyenay around that they both had bananas growing all over them. It hadn't gone quite as they'd planned, but then not even gods can plan for a completely hilarious night out. Sometimes they just happen.

The Price of
True Beauty

With a heavy trudge, the six slaves heaved the sedan sofa along the track past the Unsightly Hills of Napp. It wasn't nearly so much fun now that Urgum had cleared the nappars out. They used to enjoy returning home carrying their over-rich passengers with their pants stuffed in their mouths. The stuffed pants stopped them screeching and moaning for one thing, unlike today when *she* hadn't shut up the whole way.

"They really should do something with this desert," she was saying. "A carpet or something would brighten it up. And why aren't there shops? Supposing I was stuck out here alone and helpless on a blazing hot day – what am I supposed to do if my hat suddenly goes out of fashion?" A thin whip cracked across the neck of the leading slave. "Faster! This really is too unbearable." The slaves were about to break into a run when: "Stop, you fools!" So they stopped. Now what?

"Thank goodness!" she said. "At least someone's had the sense to put up an emergency mirror." *A mirror?* thought the slaves, looking round in amazement. But sure enough, there, standing slap-bang exactly in the middle of nowhere, was a mirror.

"Well?" She lashed out with the whip again. "Lower me down!"

The slaves lowered the sedan sofa to the ground. "I'll just refresh myself with a glimpse of true beauty before we continue." Her dainty rhino-horn shoes clicked down on to the desert rock. "And don't you *dare* walk off with that empty sofa."

With that, she wrapped her peacock feather cloak around her shoulders and tottled towards the mirror.

Meanwhile, a tiny creature had hopped between the feet of the leading slave, looking for something comfortable to lie on. It looked up and saw it, hopped up and

landed on it, curled up, took a *deeep* breath, put its feet in its mouth and fell asleep. The slaves noticed that there wasn't a gap on the sofa any more. So it wasn't empty. So they could go. So off they went.

Meanwhile, somewhere far away, Orgo and the Gorgos were happily picking bananas from trees, flowers, snakes, zebras, frogs and worms, and stuffing them into their mouths as fast as they could.

Ding-a-ling!

U rgum woke up with a start. Forgetting that he wasn't in bed, he rolled over to give Divina a squeeze, and fell off the high ledge at the top of the cragg. Luckily, he didn't drop straight to the ground below, instead there were lots of sharp bits of rock sticking out for him to bump into on the way down.

He sat up and spat a few loose teeth out. His head was spinning, he was covered in cuts, bruises, sores and grazes, but he was still alive. Eeek! Even when Divina was in a bad mood, squeezing her wasn't as dangerous as that. Well, not quite. He rubbed his eyes and remembered he was sulking and why, and then realized that he had woken up because the bell had *ding-a-linged*. Something had fallen into his trap! He looked over to the Wandering Jungle … then rubbed his eyes again. He opened one eye, then shut it and tried the other one. Then he tried them both at once, but got the same result. No Wandering Jungle, for some reason it had wandered off! He staggered to his feet and dragged himself over to where the jungle had been. There were a few scuff marks on the ground and a squashed ant with a bunch of bananas growing on its leg, but otherwise it was just the usual desert rock again. Over in the distance Divina's mirror was standing slap-bang in the middle of nowhere. As he went over to get it, his brain dived back into the ocean of sulk, but then suddenly the ocean of sulk went gurgling away down the plughole of smugness. Yippee – there was something in the trap!

Urgum hoisted the creature out. It was covered from head to foot in black tar with a few horrible feathers sticking out, and it was making the most dreadful screeching noises. Sadly, it was far too weedy to be Orgo himself, but it would do to start with. Even though Urgum's head was still woozy from his fall, he managed a gloating smirk as he limped back to the cragg, shoving his captive in front of him. As they went in past Olk ("Password" … "Enormous strawberry fool ice cream" … "Enter") the giant licked his lips. To Olk, a bit of tar was just like extra gravy.

Inside the cragg, the seven savage sons were lounging around on the rocks busy doing nothing.

"Ooh look, Dad's come down off his ledge," said Robbin.

"What have you got there?" asked Ruinn.

"A gorgo!" said Urgum, wiping some blood from his face where one of the cliff rocks had bashed him.

"You look well damaged!" said Rekk.

"That thing must have put up a super fight!" said Rakk.

"Er … well yes, it did its best," grinned Urgum. "But I'm the fiercest savage in the desert and don't you forget it. Yarghhh!"

Divina was glad to hear Urgum yarghhhing, it meant he'd stopped sulking, so she came out of the cave to meet him. "Ah, Divina!" he shouted proudly. "I've got a little present for you."

"I don't want that filthy thing in here," said Divina.

"Oh yes you do," said Urgum. "You can clean it up and then it's going to be that slave you wanted."

"My own slave?"

"No!" screeched the creature.

"It speaks!" exclaimed Divina happily. She was already imagining having nice polite conversations while watching her kitchen being scrubbed out.

"I will NEVER be a slave!" said the creature.

"Good for you," said Urgum, impressed. "Slaving isn't for everybody, so if you've got your pride, I respect that. You can choose, do you want to be a slave or something else?"

"Something else!"

"Come on then."

Urgum took the creature back out to the giant sentry. The boys watched him still limping. Whatever that thing was, it had really hurt him!

"Olk likes gorgos, don't you, Olk? So how do you fancy this one?"

Olk's eyes fluttered open and looked downwards. His great nose sniffed, then wrinkled. His mouth opened in a huge hungry grin and his tongue rolled out down his chest.

"Roasted," said Olk.

Urgum smiled at the creature. "Your choice. You can either be Divina's slave or Olk's lunch."

"No, no!" screamed the captive, breaking free from Urgum. It ran back to the cave and fell at Divina's feet.

"Please! I'll be your slave, please, I beg you!"

"Hmmm, maybe," said Divina. "You can carry in the water and firewood."

"Oh, I can't do lifting," said the slave. "I've never lifted anything in my life."

"Then you'll have to do cleaning."

"You mean I touch dirt? Oh no, I'd die!"

"Then what can you do? Round here if you can't do anything, you're food."

"Argh!" the slave shrieked. "How about, er …
maybe … oh I know! I can shop."

"Shop?"

"Oh yes, I can try on things all day, especially shoes.
And I'm really good at sending things back, and in fact
my speciality is complaining about nothing. I often have
slaves whipped for no reason at all!"

"Oh really?" Divina was starting to peer at this strange
creature more carefully. "You must tell me more about
whipping slaves, bearing in mind you've just begged to
be *my* slave."

"Oh no … but but but …"

Just then Molly turned up with a bowl of water.

"Does it know how to wash?" asked Molly.

"Oh I think so," said Divina. "Don't you Suprema?"

Meanwhile, the boys had gathered round Urgum so
he could give them a guided tour of all his new injuries.

"That's where it thumped me …"

"Cool!"

"… and that's a big gash from one of its talons …"

"Cool!"

"… and here's where it tried to bite my leg off …"

"Cool!"

But Ruff had got a bit bored of Urgum getting all the

attention and looked round just in time to see Molly tipping the water over Suprema's head.

"Hey, look!" he shouted.

The boys all watched in amazement as the worst of the sloppy tar washed away.

"That's not a gorgo," said Ruinn. "It's a softhand!"

"A posh woman softhand has beaten Dad up!" said Ruff.

"What?" gasped Urgum.

"HA HA HA HA HA!" laughed the boys. "So much for the fiercest savage the Lost Desert has ever known."

"But … but actually I fell off the ledge."

"Oh yeah yeah," chortled the chaps. "Tripped on your own shadow too, eh?"

They all pointed at Urgum and chanted, "Urgum is a loser, Urgum is a loser …"

Urgum turned his back on them and hobbled painfully away. The ocean of sulk was waiting for him, deeper and glueyer than ever.

There was panic up in the Halls of Sirrus. Tangor and Tangal had happily been eating the bananas off each other until they were disturbed by the sons' chanting.

"This is really bad!" said Tangal. "If only he'd caught

Orgo, he'd have transferred all his sulk into fight energy and been absolutely unbeatable. We'd have got our champion back bigger and more unbearably proud than ever."

"It's our fault for upsetting the Wandering Jungle," said Tangor. "It felt silly covered in bananas. No wonder it ran off."

"I've never seen a barbarian sulk this deep before," said Tangor. "You don't think it could be ... fatal?"

"Oh don't!" cried Tangal.

It was a scary thought. When true barbarians died, they were entitled to join the gods and feast on divine nectar for eternity. This was extremely hard work for the gods, but so long as the barbarian had died in a truly glorious and gruesome way, at least it would make for a reasonably jolly afterlife party. But what would it be like forever feeding divine nectar to a barbarian who had died of terminal sulking?

"If he goes on like this, I think I'd prefer it if the accountancy gods did get him," groaned Tangor.

"But he's our last true barbarian," said Tangal. "Without him, we'll stop being gods. We'll just be little floaty things drifting round the sky like a slightly iffy smell for eternity."

Even with all their divine power, the twin gods had completely run out of ideas. They could only look down as their fate was decided by the fortunes of mortals, but fortunately for them, there was one mortal who wasn't going to give up on Urgum quite so easily.

Back by the cave Suprema was hissing and fizzing like a snake with its tail trapped in an oven door. Divina was trying hard not to laugh. "Oh, wait till I tell the others that you begged to be my slave!"

"Don't you dare. Don't you *dare*!"

"What was it you said to me?" said Divina. "'… if you please me I won't have you whipped too hard' …?"

"Mum!" Molly was pointing at Urgum, who had gone to sit huddled up in a dark corner of the cave and feel sorry for himself. "Dad's gone off again! He's really gone."

For a moment Divina forgot about Suprema. "Oh dear! He's taken this gorgo thing very badly."

"He's still the fiercest savage in the Lost Desert, isn't he, Mum?"

"Of course!" said Divina. "You know that, I know that."

"I know what would cheer him up," said Molly. "Suppose *everybody* knew it?"

"Just so long as nobody knows about me!" snapped Suprema. "If you people dare to breathe a word …"

"Don't flatter yourself," said Molly. "We've got better things to talk about than you. But you've got to do something for us."

"What?"

"*Modern Savage* magazine is having the Savvy awards soon. MY dad is going to be the Savage of the Year!"

"Why?" snapped Suprema.

"Because he IS and always has been."

"So why hasn't he ever won it?"

Divina explained. "That's only because he refuses to have anything to do with money. Every year he's passed by for someone who bribes the judges."

"Well, of course! It's the tradition," said Suprema.

"But this year, he's going to win," said Molly.

"But what happens if somebody bribes the judges?" asked Suprema.

"Well, duh!" said Molly. "Of course somebody's going to bribe the judges. YOU."

Tangor and Tangal heaved a huge sigh of relief. Thank goodness for Molly! If Urgum won the Savage of the Year award, he'd be far too unbearably smug to die of sulking. It was the perfect answer to all their worries, apart from one tiny hitch. Urgum was supposed to be their barbarian champion, so he should be winning that award by fighting gloriously and gruesomely for it. He should NOT be having it bought for him by the softest softhand that the Lost Desert has ever known. Oh dear, what would the other gods say? It could all end up being squirmily embarrassing. Urk!

But then the divine twins realized that the tiny hitch wasn't going to happen. After all, they were dealing with *Urgum*. He was about to go to a massive party packed with all the nastiest savages of the Lost Desert. Was it possible that he could turn up, sit down, behave himself, modestly accept the top prize and quietly come away without having a glorious and gruesome fight with someone? Absolutely no way.

All Tangor and Tangal had to do to get Urgum back to his good old barbaric self was to make sure he got to those awards. They knew they could rely on his endearing brutality to do the rest.

The Unwanted Invitation

GOYANGGGGG! It was a few days later that the sound crashed through the blistering sunlight and bounced around the baking rocks of Golgarth basin before barging into the cave, whooshing down the passageway, screeching into the bedroom and landing in Divina's ear. It was just the sound she'd been waiting for – she'd been madly rearranging her dressing table, because at last she knew was going to get something really fabulously exquisite to go in the gap.

"The door chime!" She winked at Molly, who'd been invited to help so long as she didn't touch anything. "Now I wonder, whatever could that be for?"

Actually they both knew exactly what it was for, and Molly hurried out of the cave and across to the cragg entrance where Olk had just smashed the giant gong beside him with his elephant-stunning mallet. She came back with a little golden box to find Divina waiting in the lounge. Urgum was still sitting in the corner sulking about gorgos, miracle mini-clubs, clever daughters, useless traps, Wandering Forests that just wandered off, tar-covered softhands, falling off ledges and being called a loser. Like the others, he knew exactly what was in the little golden box, and he also knew it was just one more thing to sulk about.

"How exciting!" said Divina, winking at Molly again.

"It's for you, Dad," said Molly, poking him with the box. "Grizelda got one too."

"Go on then, Urgie, open it!" gushed Divina.

Urgum crossly brushed the box away with his hand and Divina snatched it.

"All right, I'll do it if you insist," she said. Inside was a neat little card. "Oh, Urgie! You've been invited to the Savvy awards ceremony at The Laplace Party Temple, sponsored by *Modern Savage* magazine."

"Big deal," muttered Urgum. "I'm not going."

"But Urgie …"

"Don't tell me, I've been nominated to win the Savage of the Year award … again."

"That's the top award, Dad," said Molly, winking at Divina.

"Urgie, you've got to go!" said Divina. "It'll cheer you up."

"I don't need cheering up," snapped Urgum.

"You do," said Molly.

"NO I DON'T BECAUSE I'M VERY HAPPY AS I AM THANK YOU VERY MUCH NOW GO AWAY."

Divina was starting to panic. It wasn't just a matter of cheering Urgum up, it was also a matter of dressing tables, gaps and fabulously exquisite little golden statuettes. "Urgie, please go, because this time you might, ahem … *bring something home*."

"What's so special about this time?" said Urgum. "I'm sick of the Savvy awards. They invite you there, make you sit still for ages and then tell you that somebody else has won and then they expect you not to kill them."

"But Urgie ..." said Divina.

"No!"

"Oh, but Dad ..." said Molly.

"NO!"

On the other side of Golgarth basin, Grizelda had reacted slightly differently when one of her meebobs had collected her little golden box from Olk and delivered it to her.

"WHOO! WOW! Who's the TOP GIRL? Walla-walla-WHOOP!"

Grizelda was kissing her little gold box and leaping up and down in front of her cave, kicking her legs out all over the place. Or at least she was until she saw that Mungoid was sitting outside his cave on something purple and lumpy. He was staring at her, so immediately she shut up and looked at her foot crossly.

"I mean 'ow'," she said sharply. "Ow. Just trod on an old cactus spike. Ow."

"Is that an invite to the Savvys?" asked Mungoid.

"What, this?" said Grizelda, desperately trying to be cool. "Oh yeah. I've been nominated for something or other."

"Well done!" beamed Mungoid. "Best archer? Most lethal assassin?"

Grizelda shook her head. "No way, matey! It's not one of those piffling, made-up, time-filling, everybody-has-to-get-something-and-go-home-happy awards. This is one of the biggies."

"Wow! What?"

"It's *only* the ..." Grizelda took a deep breath and tried to calm herself, "... Most Unexpectedly Nice Hair on a Very Dangerous Person award."

"Good one!" said Mungoid, licking his hand and smoothing down his three hairs. "I wouldn't mind winning that myself."

"Yeah, well," said Grizelda. "I might win, I might not. Couldn't care, actually, but I don't want to bother going if not. I'd better find out."

She pinged the bell that hung outside her cave and immediately a little hairy meebob appeared. "Hurry up, hurry UP!" she hissed as the meebob scuttled off to get her horse.

"How can you find out?" asked Mungoid. "The results

are all kept secret until the night."

"Oh pul-ease," said Grizelda. "When you happen to know the committee scribe's brother, you can find out anything. Especially if you're a very dangerous person with unexpectedly nice hair."

The purple thing that Mungoid was sitting on started to wriggle, so with a heavy sigh he stood up. Abill struggled to his feet and smoothed down his shabby robes. "Now then, where was I?" he said. "Had I mentioned the day of my birth? My mother had already born forty-nine other children whose names were *floobah mmmpph...*"

Mungoid wrapped his huge hand around Abill's mouth as the meebob returned with Grizelda's horse. She backflipped herself on to it, her long flame-coloured locks swishing around in a perfect circle as she did so. Mungoid's jaw dropped open in admiration.

"And keep tomorrow night free," said Grizelda. "I need to take a guest if I'm going, so it may as well be you. But it's all a bit boring really. Hopefully I'm not going to win, then I don't have to go. But I don't care, see? So that's that."

Grizelda galloped off and away through the gateway past Olk.

"Snurt," said the meebob.

"...thumumf..." agreed Abill.

"Yeah, that's what I think too," grinned Mungoid. Of course she cared!

Back in Urgum's cave, Molly was flicking through the latest copy of *Modern Savage* magazine.

"Dad!" she said. "You've got to go because you ARE going to win. I've just realized, it's in here somewhere."

Urgum groaned. He truly did not like *Modern Savage* magazine. Divina was always reading it and getting wistful ideas on what colour she wanted her hair and dreaming of holidays that didn't involve fighting. Molly shoved an open page in front of Urgum.

"There!" she said and showed him a grid of letters.

WORDSEARCH

Who will win
Savage of the Year?

Can you find the name of a legendary barbarian in the grid? Names may read horizontally, vertically or diagonally.

```
Q U Q Q Q Q Q
Q R Q Q Q Q Q
Q G Q Q Q Q Q
Q U Q Q Q Q Q
Q M Q Q Q Q Q
Q Q Q Q Q Q Q
```

"Don't you see?" shouted Molly excitedly. "It's a puzzle to tell who the winner will be, and the answer is YOU, Dad! There's your name."

"I can't see it," said Urgum, which was quite true because he couldn't read.

"You're just being difficult," said Molly. "What does it take to convince you?"

"Huh!" sniffed Divina. "You'll be lucky." With a deep sigh she went back to her bedroom and tried not to look at the gap on the dressing table.

Molly was left staring at Urgum so crossly that he felt he had to explain. He went over to an alcove in which sat two small statues of the gods Tangor and Tangal.

"Get real, Molly," said Urgum. "I'm not going to win, and that's all there is to it. And I refuse to embarrass our barbarian twin gods by even thinking about it."

Urgum turned away just too early to see the little statues turn to face each other.

"But this year he *is* going to win!" hissed Tangor.

"Of course, Suprema's bribed absolutely everybody," said Tangal. "And once he's got the award, he'll stop sulking and we can try and put our lives back to normal!"

"But he'll only get the award if he turns up," said Tangor. "How can we make sure he gets there?"

The little statues suddenly froze again as Molly came over and stared at them. "If only the gods could send you a divine sign," she sighed, tapping the little Tangor statue's head.

"… eee-oooch!" said Tangor, gritting his teeth. That hurt!

"She's right," whispered Tangal to her brother. "All Urgum needs is a divine sign. Come on."

Nobody noticed the little statues mysteriously disappear. Instead, Molly went to watch Urgum prodding the fire.

"Divine sign!" Urgum muttered. "And exactly what's one of those then?"

In answer to his question, the flames of the fire suddenly twisted themselves altogether and formed a perfect replica of a glittering gold Savvy award.

"Dad!" cried Molly excitedly. "Look, doesn't that look like a Savvy award to you?"

"How would I know?" said Urgum, unimpressed. "I've never had one, remember?"

"But that's got to be a divine sign!" insisted Molly.

"Pah!" scoffed Urgum. He slammed his axe into the fire, making the flames shoot all over the place in a shower of sparks. "Call that a sign? It was just a few flames getting stuck together. If I'm really going to win this award the gods'll have to do a better sign than that."

From inside the fire Tangor and Tangal exchanged glances and sighed. This was going to be tougher than they thought.

"All right," said Molly. "I'm sure the gods can come up with something else."

"Oh yeah?" said Urgum. "Like what?"

The second sign began as a hissing noise that came from outside the cave. An army of golden cobras writhed in through the door towards them, while a nest of green mambas dropped from the roof and a selection of other lethal snakes burrowed their way up through the sand by their feet. Within a few seconds the floor in front of them was covered in slim writhing bodies and soon they had wriggled into position to form a giant pattern perfectly illustrating the shape and colours of a Savvy award. If only Urgum could have read it, a line of small black sand asps along the bottom had twisted themselves into the letters *Savvy*. Gradually the snakes all fell still and silent, their skins glistening in the sunlight from the cave entrance.

"There!" said Molly. "How about that?"

"Pah," said Urgum. "Call that a sign? I call it a snack."

Urgum grabbed one of the mambas, twisted its head off and prepared to take a bite from the twitching neck, but at once the snakes all disappeared into a thin mist which quickly drifted away in the evening breeze.

"In fact it's not even a snack," said Urgum after his jaw had snapped shut on thin air.

"Oh, for the sake of the gods!" blasted Molly. "You – come with me."

"Where?" said Urgum, quickly followed by "Yowk, stoppit!"

Molly grabbed Urgum by the ear and dragged him backwards right down the lounge, out of the cave, right across the basin to the steps leading up to the cragg watchtower post, all the way up to the top and then yanked his head round to face the smoking volcano on the distant horizon. Molly then took a deep breath and in a voice shrill enough to make all the teeth chatter down Smiley Alley she screamed:

"Oh, great gods! I demand you give us a final sign. Will Urgum win this Savvy award thing?"

At once the volcano erupted with a deafening BOOM, spewing jets of flame and black smoke far up into the evening sky. Streams of white-hot lava gushed down the sides while the earth shook, the valleys

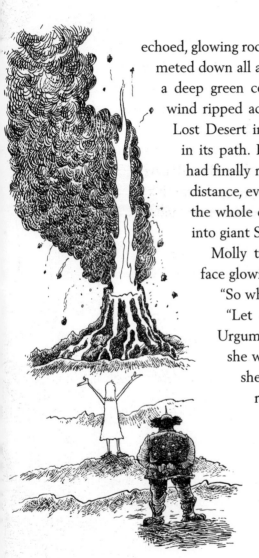

echoed, glowing rocks and boulders plummeted down all around, the sun turned a deep green colour and a blistering wind ripped across the plains of the Lost Desert incinerating everything in its path. By the time the noise had finally rumbled away into the distance, every single cloud across the whole desert sky had formed into giant Savvy award shapes.

Molly turned to Urgum, her face glowing in triumph.

"So what do you say now?"

"Let go of my ear!" said Urgum. Molly had forgotten she was still clutching it, so she let go and Urgum reached up to see if it was still connected to his head.

"But what about the sign?"

"What sign?" said Urgum.

"You mean the my-ear-hurts sign?"

"Oh, GET OVER IT, you boring old boring lump of boringness!" she cried. "I asked the gods if you were going to win and immediately the volcano exploded."

"Pah! Was that supposed to be a sign?" asked Urgum. "Then they should have made it clearer. Ask them again, and this time make it one BOOM for yes and two BOOMS for no."

"No," said Molly simply. She took a deep breath and steadied her temper. "I give in. If you're going to be like that then BE like that. What's the point? Forget it."

"You know your trouble?" said Urgum. "You give up too easily."

Molly stomped back to their cave in silence, followed by Urgum, but just then Grizelda rode in. She leapt off her horse and threw her

I can't believe it's not LAVA

213

invitation at Mungoid, who was sitting on Abill again.

"There, you have it!" she said. "I'm not going."

"Why not?" asked Mungoid.

"I just happen to be very busy, actually," snapped Grizelda. "So I'm not going and I don't care."

She was just about to stomp into her cave when she spotted Urgum. "CHEAT!" she screamed.

"Eh?" said Urgum. "You talking to me?"

"Well, I don't see any other cheats round here," said Grizelda, pretending to look round. Finally, she glared at Urgum so hard that his skin started to peel. "Don't play dumb. You must have cheated if they're giving you the Savage of the Year award."

"Me?" gasped Urgum.

"Yeah yeah yeah, you!" said Grizelda. "Everyone knows but no one's supposed to tell you because it's meant to be a big surprise, but of course you know anyway because you cheated because you're a cheat."

Grizelda stomped into her cave leaving Urgum standing dumbstruck.

"Wow!" he finally said to himself. "If Grizelda says I've got it, then … I'VE GOT IT!"

Equine Revenge

On the morning of the awards ceremony, Urgum, Molly, Divina and the seven sons were sitting in the kitchen getting excited.

"Gosh, I'm getting excited," said Molly.

"Let's hear your acceptance speech again, dear," said Divina.

"Ahem..." said Urgum clearing his throat. "YARGHH-HHH!"

"That's good, Dad!" said Molly. "Very good."

"Now then, you must look your best for the awards!" fussed Divina. "Make sure they know that you're the fiercest savage that the Lost Desert has ever known. Let me help."

"How can you help?" asked Urgum.

Divina took a hippo-gutting ladle from a hook on the wall. She swung it round her head with both hands and slammed it into Urgum's eye.

WOLLUTCH!

"There, that's better!" said Divina, hanging the ladle up again. "It'll bruise up nicely by this evening."

"He still looks a bit soft!" said Ruff.

"Right!" agreed Ruinn. "Can't have our dad looking soft." Immediately, Urgum's loyal sons ran at him swinging their fists and gnashing their teeth. One mighty punch-up later...

"Pah!" shouted Urgum, standing on top of a heap of beaten sons. "Call that a fight? It's a bit sad when I can take on all my seven sons at once."

"That's not fair," muttered Ruinn, pointing to the pile of bags in the corner. "Raymond wasn't fighting."

Urgum went over to the bags. "That's because at least Raymond has a bit of respect for his father."

But then a leg stuck out from one of the bags and hoofed Urgum WALLOP under the chin. Urgum staggered backwards, caught his heel on the edge of the fire

grate and sat down on the burning logs.

"YOW!" yelped Urgum, leaping up.

"Hurrah for Raymond!" cheered the others.

"And now you're looking much tougher," said Molly. "Especially with that smoke coming from your bottom."

"Oh no!" said Urgum. "My bottom's on fire!"

"What?" gasped Ruinn. "ALL of it? Quick, put it out before the whole desert goes up."

Urgum dashed over to the rock pool in the corner and sat in it. There was a sharp sizzling noise and wafts of steam arose around him. A relieved smile spread across his face.

"Phew!" he said. "That's better."

"Molly," said Divina, "call Grizelda. She better come and have look at it."

"What?" retorted Urgum. "No way is Grizelda looking at my bottom."

"Don't be such a baby," said Divina. "Besides you might need some of her healing potion on it."

"What?" blushed Urgum. "I can't have her putting cream on my bottom! What will she say?"

"We know what she *won't* say!" giggled Ruinn.

"She won't say it's small," said Rekk.

"And she won't say it's pretty," said Rakk.

And indeed when Grizelda came along she did not say Urgum's bottom was small or pretty. What she *did* say was:

"Serves you right for cheating."

"But I never cheated!" said Urgum, who was bending over at the time.

"So you're calling me a liar, are you?" asked Grizelda. "Oh, I've just remembered. This bottom cream only works if it's very boiling."

"Very boiling?" asked Urgum. "You mean boiling hot?"

Grizelda had already poured some light-blue liquid into a metal pan and thrust it into the fire.

"Of course she means boiling hot," laughed Ruff. "There's no such thing as boiling cold."

"HO HO HO," laughed all the boys, but Grizelda silenced them with a stern look.

"If you people don't take this treatment seriously, I won't do it," she warned them. The boys immediately took it very seriously. Pouring very boiling cream on to their father's bottom was a serious business.

"That's better," said Grizelda. "But this bottom cream needs rubbing in with a leaf from the spiky cactus plant. Any volunteers?"

Within seconds the sons had dashed out and grabbed the spikiest cactus leaves and soon they were rubbing them as hard as they could on Urgum's blistered bottom.

"Don't forget the cream, boys!" grinned Grizelda, but nobody could hear her over Urgum's yelps of pain.

Soon everybody was outside organizing the horses and getting ready to go. Only Grizelda was standing to one side looking very left out. "I hope you all have a VERY nice time then," she said. "Especially the CHEAT."

"Aren't you coming, Grizelda?" asked Molly. "It'll be fun!"

"Fun for some," snapped Grizelda, running her fingers through her hair sadly.

"Come on, Grizelda," said Divina. "You can sit with us."

"No she can't," jeered Ruff. "We don't sit with LOSERS."

"HA HA HA," laughed all the boys.

Grizelda was about to give Ruff one of her killer glares, but suddenly her lip quivered. She put her hands to her face and ran away into her cave. Divina took over the glaring duties for her, and even raised her left eyebrow a tiny fraction. Ruff went bright crimson and the other boys all backed away.

"What?" bleated Ruff.

"I shan't be going either," said Divina.

"Why?" said Urgum.

Divina looked over to Grizelda's cave. "She might be a ruthless assassin, but she's got feelings too, you know."

"Eh?" said the boys.

Urgum was standing with his mouth open, looking bewildered. Divina stepped over and stroked his cheek. "We're lucky, Urgie, we've got family, but sometimes she gets very lonely," she said. "You lot better get off. And Molly, you make sure they all stay out of trouble. I'll get

Grizelda to show me her things from the battle market. We'll have a bit of a girls' night here, just the two of us."

"You sure?" said Urgum. "But there's bound to be some fighting and punching and blood. You'll miss it."

Divina screwed up her face in disgust, then grinned. "That's nothing compared to what you'll be missing," she said, flicking his nose with her finger.

Molly was on her horse and she trotted over to where Mungoid was climbing on to his ox. The massive face looked haggard and weary and it wasn't hard to see why.

"I haven't slept for days!" he moaned to Molly.

"Wherever I am, whatever I'm doing ... *he's* there!"

And sure enough, standing behind the great ox was Abill in his shabby purple robes looking anxiously at Mungoid. As soon as Mungoid caught his eye he continued talking:

"Now then, where did I get to?"

"I don't know where you got to," muttered Mungoid, clutching the invitation Grizelda had thrown him. "But me, I'm getting away!"

"Oh dear," said Abill. "Had we done the port of Genza when the rest of my family were on the boat and they asked me to step ashore to undo the rope and before I knew it the boat had pulled away and I had to swim to catch up?"

"I can't remember," moaned Mungoid.

"Oh," said Abill. "There's just one thing for it then. I better start again."

"Oh no!" wailed Mungoid.

"I don't mind, honest!" said Abill. "So once again I must take you back to the day of my birth. My mother had already born forty-nine other children whose names were..."

"Why don't you throttle him?" whispered Molly.

"It'd just give him more to talk about," sighed

Mungoid. "Never mind. Let's just go. He'll never catch up with us on foot."

As they all rode out of the cragg, Urgum's horse was rather puzzled. For once Fatty hadn't run up and tried to jump on, instead he had climbed up extremely carefully and had lowered himself very slowly on to the horse's back. The horse couldn't understand this at all until it heard Grizelda call out from the watchtower: "Now do take extra care of that bottom of yours, Urgum. Otherwise it will be VERY sore."

The horse found this very interesting and decided to try a little experiment. It broke into a little gallop, deliberately bouncing up and down more than necessary. A satisfying selection of whimpers and curses came from Fatty, which gave the horse an even better idea.

"YARGHHH!" the seven sons cheered as they galloped ahead, kicking up a cloud of dust.

"Come on, Dad," said Molly. "We'd better keep up!"

"I'm doing my best!" hissed Urgum. He gritted his teeth as he tried to ease his horse into going a bit faster, but the horse seemed to be adding an extra merry little bounce with every single step. Molly and Urgum followed behind, watching curiously.

"Molly," said Mungoid, sounding concerned. "There's

something odd going on. I've seen horses trot, gallop, walk, canter and jump, but is it me, or is Urgum's horse … skipping?"

And the Winner Is...

The Laplace Party Temple was the most magnificent place in the Lost Desert. It had been built well away from the main Laplace Palace so that the noise wouldn't keep any hard-working softhands awake at night (just in case the day ever came that a softhand actually worked hard). The entire building had been carved out of one single giant ruby, and as Urgum and everybody all headed across the sands of the desert towards it, they felt like they were riding across the top of a gigantic cherry cake to the cherry in the middle. They tied up their horses outside the deep red battlements, then stepped through the outer gates and entered the courtyard. As they made their way across to the great hall, Molly was absolutely stunned. Everything she looked at, the walls, the floors, the pillars, the steps, the whole lot was ruby red. In the centre of the courtyard was a ruby fountain and even the water that was happily gurgling and slapping about in the pool at the bottom looked like blood.

It was almost a relief when something appeared that wasn't red. They had just got past the fountain, when a small man in a huge hat stepped out in front of them. He was wearing the green and gold uniform of the palace guard.

"Wait a minute!" said the small man.

"Hunjah the Headless!" said Urgum. "Are you supposed to be a palace guard now?"

"Absolutely," said Hunjah. "And I've got to tell you not to take your weapons in."

"Ho ho ho!" laughed the seven sons.

"I'm warning you!" insisted Hunjah. "We've got a lodestone fitted."

"A what?" grumped Urgum.

"A lodestone," called Hunjah, as they all barged past him. "So no weapons. I mean it, honest!"

But they had already shoved past him and were heading towards the archway that lead into the hall.

"What's a lodestone, Dad?" asked Robbin.

"It's a load of rubbish," laughed Urgum.

When they got to the archway, they looked up to see the roof of the arch was almost completely covered in swords, axes, shields, maces and daggers.

"Wow!" said Ruff. "Look at all that good gear. What's it doing floating up there?"

The twins had spotted a particularly fine needle sabre dangling down from the pile.

"Mine!" they both shouted, and then, "I'll fight you for it!"

They ran under the archway drawing their swords, but then the strangest thing happened.

CLONK CLANG. Both their swords shot from their hands and flew upwards to stick on the archway roof. The twins frantically jumped up to try and grab them back, but they were well out of reach.

"Dad!" they wailed. "It's witchcraft!"

"I tried to tell you," called Hunjah from behind them. "There's a giant lodestone built into the archway. Anything with metal won't get past, so don't try it."

Under the arch the twins were starting to argue.

"Let me climb up on your shoulders," said Rakk to Rekk. "Then I can reach my sword and then I can kill you."

."No way!" snapped Rekk. "I'm not having your smelly feet on my shoulders. YOU get on MY shoulders."

"Behave, you two!" snapped Urgum, stepping towards the arch. Immediately he felt his axe come alive in his hands. It was as if an invisible rope was trying to haul the axe head up to the roof. Urgum was completely mystified, but he was determined to get his axe into the palace. With all his might he clung on to the axe handle and tried to drag it down to the ground as he stepped under the arch.

"Let go of my axe!" he shouted desperately into thin air. It didn't do him any good.

WHEEE-KADDANG!

The axe suddenly shot up to the roof of the arch so fast that Urgum didn't have time to let go of the handle. The boys all gathered underneath to see his legs helplessly kicking about in the air.

"Get me down!" demanded Urgum crossly.

"Just let go then," said Rakk.

"We'll catch you," said Rekk. They stood underneath him with arms outstretched.

"Promise?" said Urgum, letting go.

"No," said Rakk and Rekk, stepping backwards.

CAR-RUNCH... Urgum landed full smack on his tender bottom.

"Ooyah! You putrid pair of pig snots," cursed Urgum as he staggered to his feet and limped after the others into the hall.

The great hall of the palace was lit by hundreds of flaming torches all round the deep red walls. Scores of tables covered the floor around which all the roughest and nastiest savages of the desert were gathered. Urgum and the others found an empty table near the stage, but just as they sat down a loud jeer came from nearby.

"It's Urgum the fatman!" came Orgo the Gorgo's voice.

"It's Mr Fatman to you, bird-head," said Urgum.

Molly looked over to see Orgo and a shabby gaggle of other gorgos clustered round a table.

"What are you doing here, loser?" shouted Orgo.

"He's getting an award," said Molly.

"Oh he is, is he?" replied Orgo.

"It's a surprise," said Molly.

"Oh, he'll be surprised all right," said Orgo and then he and the others laughed the foul laugh of the gorgos: "*cakka cakka cakka.*"

"That does it," said Urgum, rising to his feet. "I'm going to change the shape of your head."

"Yeah! Do it, Dad!" cheered the seven sons.

"Dad!" said Molly, urgently tugging his arm. "Save it for later. Remember how much Mum wants the award."

"Hmph," muttered Urgum. Forgetting how raw his bottom was, he sat down with a bump which made him remember again.

"Yeooowwww...!" he cried.

"Something the matter, Urgum?" grinned Orgo.

Urgum was still yowing but realized he needed to disguise it.

"...owwww long is it until these awards start then?" he asked.

"Soon," said Molly.

Mungoid had been to collect some drinks and arrived at the table clutching a very large jug and several goblets.

"Here," said Mungoid. "Forget Orgo, let's have some punch instead."

"Is that the stuff from the punch fruit that tastes like a punch in the mouth?" said Molly.

"Absolutely," said Mungoid.

"How totally vommo!" said Molly. "Not for me, thanks."

"Hooray!" said the boys. "All the more for us."

"Go steady with that stuff," warned Mungoid, but too late. The goblets were poured.

"Let's drink to Dad getting the prize," said Ruff.

"Forget that," said Ruinn. "Let's drink to Dad's sore bottom."

"Hooray!" cheered the boys. "Bottoms up." They all emptied their goblets at once.

"Wow!" said Ruinn with his eyes rolling. "It *does* taste like a punch in the ..."

^CLUNK

All seven boys' heads hit the table together and started snoring immediately.

TUB-ARP TUB-ARP

A fanfare of trumpets sounded and then a very elegant lady in a green and gold velvet dress stepped out from behind the mammoth-skin curtains at the side of the stage. She had perfect straight white hair and huge eyes that could swivel round and point in different directions, but that wasn't the best bit.

"She's got a tail!" whispered Molly excitedly.

Indeed, as the lady walked across to the centre of the stage, it was just possible to make out a green scaly tail tucked neatly beneath the folds of the dress.

"She's a dizzalid," said Urgum approvingly. "Part woman, part lizard and as tough as they come. You need to be for this lot," he added, indicating the leering savages filling the hall.

"They're good kissers too," said Mungoid.

"Mungoid!" giggled Molly. "What did you just say?"

"N ... nothing," replied Mungoid hurriedly.

Slowly, the dizzalid cast her gaze around the room, and for a second those huge eyes locked on to Mungoid, making him blush furiously and look down at his knees. With the faintest of smiles and a flick of her black-forked tongue she began to address the crowd in a beautiful and powerful voice.

"Good evening and welcome to the Savvy awards," she announced to a massive cheer. "I am Mulma, your hostess for the evening, but before we start with the awards, we are delighted to entertain you with the hottest cabaret act of the desert, the Flying Choppas."

To a roar of applause a huge savage ran on to the stage carrying a bag full of throwing axes.

"That's unfair!" said Urgum. "How come he's allowed axes and I'm not?"

A slim woman ran on behind the first savage and tied a blindfold round his eyes, then she went over to a large board that was fixed on the wall at the back of the stage. She stood there with her arms out to the sides and shouted, "Ready!"

In a flurry of action, the blindfolded savage threw the axes one by one at the board. Each axe thudded into the board only missing the woman by a hair's breadth. At first there were massive cheers from the crowd, but gradually the cheers turned to boos. As the last axe hit the board right next to the woman's neck, the crowd were on their feet.

"USELESS! BORING! GET OFF!"

"How utterly pathetic," moaned Urgum. "He's missed with every single shot."

The axe thrower took off the blindfold and faced the audience uncertainly. As he bent over and took a deep bow the jeers and boos got even louder. Behind him the woman stepped nimbly away from the board and then, realizing the act hadn't gone well, she pulled out one of the axes. Just as the thrower straightened up, she threw it. The thrower fell forwards to the ground with the axe handle sticking from his head. The woman skipped to the front and, standing on the fallen body, she smiled and took a large bow.

"HOORAY!" everybody cheered.

"Now *that's* entertain- ment," said Urgum.

Mulma reappeared with a couple of slaves, who lugged the body from the stage and once again the room fell quiet.

"Ladies and gentlemen," she said. "We now come to the main point of the evening – the Savvy awards. Obviously you'll want to make speeches, but in case you're not sure how much to say, we've got a special timing device to help you."

Mulma pointed upwards to a heavy metal grid of spikes hanging over the stage. The grid was held in place by a rope running over a pulley, and the far end of the rope came down to the side of the stage.

"When you start your speech we put a candle under the rope," explained Mulma. "So don't go on too long or the rope will burn through and your speech will be finished for you."

A murmur of excitement went round the hall. As everyone settled down again, a slave came from behind the curtain and handed a small wooden plaque and a piece of parchment to Mulma.

"And so to our first award," said Mulma looking at the parchment. "The Savvy award for the *Best Use of Fire in a Siege Situation* goes to …"

And so one by one the awards were announced and different savages came onstage to collect them. As each savage came up, a slave placed the candle under the rope, the savage made an extremely short speech and ran off the stage and then the candle was removed again.

There did seem to be rather a lot of awards.

"What's the point of *Most Imaginative Use of a Boomerang?*" muttered Urgum.

"Or *Best Supporting Animal?*" agreed Mungoid.

However there was one presentation they had enjoyed.

"The judges couldn't decide on the *Most Intimidating Barbarian,*" explained Mulma, "but the two nominations are Junj and Xanto. However, it was decided that the award goes to ... Junj!"

A very solid-looking blue-skinned savage covered in chunky gold jewellery lumbered up on to the stage. His shoulders were almost as wide as he was tall and his fingertips came down past his ankles.

"I'll take that," he muttered, reaching a massive hand out towards the wooden plaque that Mulma was holding.

"Xanto!" said Mulma. "What are you doing? You're not Junj."

"No," said the solid savage simply. "But I had a little word with the judges and it turned out they'd got it very wrong, and they were very sorry."

"But what about Junj?" asked Mulma. "Doesn't he mind you getting the award?"

"No, I had a little word with him too and he was very reasonable about it ... eventually."

"Really?" asked Mulma.

"Ask him yourself if you like," said the savage, and then from inside the folds of his jacket he produced a severed head. "Here he is."

"Ooooh!" said the crowd.

"Hello, Junj," said Mulma to the head. "Do you mind if Xanto gets the award?"

Holding the head by the hair, Xanto moved the jaw up and down with his other hand, speaking at the same time.

"No – I – don't – mind," said Xanto, trying not to move his lips.

"Fair enough," said Mulma, shrugging her shoulders and passing the plaque over. "So the award for *Most Intimidating Barbarian* goes to Xanto."

There was a roar of approval as the huge savage turned to face the audience. The slave slipped the candle under the rope that held up the spiked grid, but when Xanto glanced in his direction he quickly moved it away again. Clasping the small wooden plaque to his chest, Xanto heaved a great sigh.

"Well," he muttered modestly. "What can a humble man say? This has come as a complete surprise, it's the last thing I expected. I just want to thank everybody who voted for me, although I can't thank the ones that didn't because they're dead."

This got a huge laugh and round of applause, but Xanto held up his great hand to restore calm.

"But most of all I want to thank my mother who's always believed in me. This one's for you, Mum. I love you and I love everybody. Thank you all so much."

Wiping a tear from his eye and waving his little wooden plaque triumphantly, he lumbered off the stage again to a mighty cheer.

"And now," continued Mulma after calm had been restored, "we come to the award for the *Most Irritating War Cry*..."

Urgum yawned and Mungoid shifted uneasily in his seat.

"When's it going to be you, Urgum?" he asked. "I can't think how this could be any more boring." And that's when it suddenly got a LOT more boring.

"There you are!" whispered a voice behind Mungoid's shoulder.

Mungoid didn't even turn his head. "Oh no, it's Abill!"

"That's me," said Abill brightly. "You're lucky I found you, because we've got a lot of catching up to do if I'm to start again. As I was saying, my mother had already borne forty-nine other children, whose names were..."

But just then Mulma's creamy voice made a special announcement.

"And now a special Savvy award for *Extracting the Most Information from a Captive* goes to ... Mungoid the Ungoid!"

Mungoid's jaw hit the table with a DUNK.

"M-me?" he muttered. Beside him Urgum and Molly were grinning.

"I got Divina to send them a message yesterday," said Urgum. "I felt you deserved something for putting up with him."

Molly was already pulling Mungoid to his feet. "Go on, go and get your award then!"

So amid a friendly chorus of cheers, boos, assorted grunts and curses Mungoid made his way to the stage and was presented with a small wooden plaque. With a nod he set off to return to his seat, but Mulma said, "You can make a speech if you like."

Mungoid stood there gobsmacked as everybody stared at him, but he got some unexpected help.

"Maybe you'd like me to say a few quick words on your behalf," said Abill, hopping up on to the stage beside him.

Mungoid nodded and returned to the table. With a smile, Mulma ushered Abill to the centre of the stage and then stepped to the side as the slave put the candle under the rope holding the metal grid.

"Ahem," began Abill. "I must congratulate Mr Ungoid for the way he forced me to talk. I had no choice but to relate my full story which began on the very day of my birth. My mother had already borne forty-nine other children, whose names were..."

Abill paused. Usually at this point he was told to shut up or he simply got slapped, but to his astonishment the crowd just sat quietly in their seats.

"What were the names?" came a voice.

"You really want to know the names?" gasped Abill.

"Yeah!" came another voice, and then more joined in.

"All forty-nine of them."

"Tell us everything!"

"Don't miss anything out."

Abill beamed with joy and faced his audience in rapture.

"Well, to cut a long story short..." he continued.

"No, don't cut it!" someone shouted.

"We want the long version!" cheered the crowd.

"Really?" exclaimed Abill. "In that case, you shall have it!"

Abill took a deep breath and started right back at the beginning. He told them *everything* about his family and how they were so proud of him that they once let him walk across a marsh first to see if it was safe, and how he was the one to test an arrow-proof vest, and how he was always chosen to be the food taster ... and all the time he could feel the crowd getting more and more excited. Abill was ecstatic. This was the very first time that he had actually been listened to, and it was the best ever moment of his tragic life. But it was also the last ever moment of his tragic life because that's when the candle burnt through the rope.

VA-BLONK!

The spiked grid plummeted down from the ceiling and into Abill. When the slaves hauled the rope to pull the grid back up with Abill impaled on it, the crowd gave their biggest cheer of the evening. He might have been dead and rather messy, but Abill still had the widest smile on his face.

"That's the way to go!" announced Mulma, walking on to the stage and carefully avoiding the blood dripping from the grid. "I'm not sure who he was, ladies and gentlemen, but I know *what* he was. He was a star!"

Everyone in the hall rose to their feet and the applause for Abill lasted nearly as long as his speech.

And the Loser Is...

There were a lot more awards to go, but Molly had noticed that Orgo had disappeared from his table.

"And now the award for the *Spikiest Hat*..." continued Mulma.

"Sounds a bit too exciting for me," said Molly to Urgum. "I'm going for a quick look round. I'll be back soon."

Mungoid and Urgum poured themselves another goblet of punch and Molly sneaked off to see what Orgo was up to. She crept behind the mammoth-skin curtain at the side of the stage and discovered a table on which the last few little wooden plaques were sitting. Beside them was a pile of small parchments. She was just about to move on when she realized somebody else was creeping about in the shadows. Molly ducked under the table and saw a pair of curious legs coming towards her. They were covered in dirty green feathers, and the feet had toes as long as fingers. There was only one savage with feet like that.

One of the small parchments fell to the floor beside her and then the feet softly shuffled away again. Molly grabbed the parchment but under the table it was too dark to read it. Just then a slave came along and took the remaining awards and parchments on to the stage. Molly slipped the dropped parchment in her pocket and crept back to rejoin Urgum and Mungoid. By the time she'd got there, the other small awards had been handed out and all that was left was a beautiful gold statuette that two slaves had brought in on a red velvet cushion.

"And finally," announced Mulma, "we come to the biggest prize of the evening. As you may know, there was a clue to who would win this next award in *Modern Savage* magazine."

Nearly every savage in the room was looking at Urgum.

"Dad!" hissed Molly urgently.

"Not now, Molly!" said Urgum. "They're coming to my turn."

"But Orgo's up to something!" she insisted.

"So what can he do? Everybody knows I'm going to win," said Urgum, then from his belt pouch he took a crumbled bit of parchment. It was the puzzle from *Modern Savage* magazine.

"Show me my name again," said Urgum.

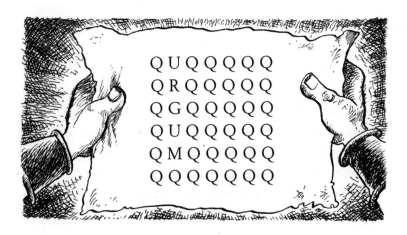

Molly pointed out the letters that spelt out "URGUM".

"I've been carrying it for luck," said Urgum. "Even Orgo can't cheat this."

"At last we can reveal the name so cleverly hidden in the word grid," said Mulma. "Ladies and gentlemen, our most prestigious award, for the Savage of the Year goes to ..."

Mulma paused. The crowd fell completely silent and everyone was looking at Urgum, who had already raised himself slightly from his seat.

"...the award goes to..."

By now Urgum was half standing up and was doing his best to pull a gosh-what-a-surprise-I-never-thought-it-would-be-me face.

"... the award goes to QGQQQQQ."

"EH?" shouted the crowd.

Urgum froze with his knees bent, bottom hovering and still wearing his gosh-what-a-surprise-I-never-thought-it-would-be-me face. In front of him a little pink creature with two huge teeth each as big as its head was crawling up on to the stage.

"Meeee!" said the creature as it strutted about in front of the crowd. "Meeee!"

"YARGGHHHH!" Urgum leapt up on the stage waving the puzzle from the magazine. "You're not the winner! In fact what ARE you?"

"It's the poppo," shouted Orgo from the audience.

"Half porcupine and half hippo, and he's called QGQQQQQ. I should know, I named him myself. Oh, and that's *Mr* QGQQQQQ to you, loser!"

"B-b-b-b-b-b-but..." said Urgum. "... but how can he be Savage of the Year? All he is is two big teeth."

"There are no special rules about teeth," said the dizzalid.

"Butty butty but but ..." Urgum was desperate, "but his name's not in the puzzle!"

"Oh yes it is," came Orgo's voice. "You should learn to read."

Urgum shoved the page of *Modern Savage* in front of the dizzalid.

"Is his name really there?" asked Urgum.

Mulma nodded and pointed to the line in the puzzle that read QGQQQQQ. Around their table Orgo and the other gorgos were laughing furiously.

"Sit down, loser," cackled Orgo. "You've never won and you never will."

Slowly and with heavy shoulders, Urgum turned to leave the stage, but as he did so Molly pushed past him.

"Stay where you are, Dad," said Molly as she ran towards Mulma. "You're the real winner and I can prove it."

It takes a lot to shock a dizzalid, but Mulma's eyes were open so wide that Molly thought they might fall out of her head. One eye was staring at the small piece of parchment she was holding herself, and with the other she read aloud what was on the piece that Molly was waving at her.

"Savage of the Year – *Urgum the Axeman*."

There was an excited murmur from the crowd and on the stage QGQQQQQ wasn't happy. With a nasty squeak he opened his mouth and advanced on Molly, but in a flash Mulma's tail whipped out from under her dress and flicked the poppo off the stage, and across the room, where it landed in Orgo's lap. The rest of Mulma had barely twitched and her tail flicked back under her dress so fast that Molly wasn't even sure if she'd really seen it happen.

"Where did you get this?" Mulma asked Molly. Her voice was quiet, but it cut so deep that every soul in the hall heard it.

"I saw someone creeping round the back of the stage," explained Molly. "He dropped it when he was swapping the parchments over."

"And who exactly did you see swapping the parchments?"

"Yes, who?" called the crowd. "Who who who?"

Molly looked out across the room. She had jumped onstage without thinking about it, but now she was aware that all the vilest and nastiest savages in the desert were staring at her. She remembered their joy when they'd seen what happened to Abill. What would they do to Orgo? Or if they liked Orgo, what would they do to her? All things considered, this had to be one of the most exciting moments of her life. She took a deep breath. Here we go...

"Orgo!" she stated loudly and proudly.

"Aha!" said everybody in the crowd at once.

"So what if I did?" sneered Orgo, climbing on to his table. Helped by a flap of his little wings he landed on the stage with one big leap. "I've had enough of this farce. Urgum's rubbish, so why give the award to him? You might just as well give it to my little friend QGQQQQQ."

"Tripe!" shouted Molly. "The only award he should get is the stupidest name award."

"But that went to Thong Thong Petticoat," said Mulma.

"So you and your friends couldn't even win that," said Molly. "Losers."

A nasty ripple of laughter came from the audience. Orgo's eyes flickered in rage and all the feathers on the back of his neck were sticking up. Even Mulma looked uncertain and took a few steps backwards.

"Listen here, little girl," snarled Orgo. "I say that award goes to the poppo."

"Oh yeah?" said Molly, looking up at the huge curved beak. "Then I'll fight you for it."

Molly put her fists up and the crowd roared its approval. But then, "You're not fighting anybody!" came a voice.

Molly saw that Urgum had arrived behind her. He tried to pull Molly away, but to his horror she refused to budge.

"Go away, Dad," hissed Molly crossly. "I'm doing fine."

"But he'll kill you!" said Urgum.

"So?" said Molly. "I'm not scared to die."

"But, but, but..." Urgum was desperate to think of something to get his stubborn daughter out of danger. Finally he blurted, "That's not the point! If you die, the poppo will get the award and then if we go home without it your mother will kill us. Think of the gap on her dressing table."

Molly thought about it. If she died, her mum would kill her. That was pretty bad. Alive or dead, it didn't do to upset Divina.

"Oh well," she said giving in. "Do your best then."

Molly hopped down from the stage to join Mungoid,

who was grinning from ear to ear.

"Listen to that!" he told her and pointed his big finger around the room. Molly hadn't noticed before, but now she realized that every savage in the place was looking her way and clapping. She covered her face in her hands. Agonizing death was no problem to Molly, but having everybody applauding was far too scary.

"It takes some nerve to face a gorgo," said Mungoid.

"Rubbish," said Molly. "I reckon I could have beaten him anyway."

"Of course you could," lied Mungoid.

TUB-ARP
TUB-ARP!

The trumpets sounded again and Mulma stepped to the front of the stage. "Ladies and gentlemen," she said. "There is only one fair way to decide who is our Savage of the Year. A duel of honour."

"Good idea!" said Urgum to Orgo. "If that poppo thing wants to be the Savage of the Year, it should come up here and fight me for it."

"No," said Orgo. "The joke's over. We both know what this is about. If you want that award, you fight me!"

"Hoorah!" cheered the crowd and immediately they all got to their feet and started throwing the tables back to clear a wide space in the middle of the hall.

"So what do you fancy?" snarled Urgum. "Swords, axes, hammers, you name it, and then say goodbye to your birdy friends. This is going to be a duel to the death!"

"To the death!" agreed Orgo.

"No," said Mulma. "Death's too easy. This calls for a duel that goes beyond death."

This was so utterly thrilling that everybody in the room took a deep breath all at once, which nearly sucked the ceiling down. Very softly, the crowd began to chant...

"Shumbitt shumbitt shumbitt..."

Urgum and Orgo glanced at each other uneasily. This was one thing that neither of them had foreseen. The chant grew louder.

"...shumbitt shumbitt SHUMBITT..."

Both Urgum and Orgo gave a shiver of terror, but Mulma was nodding in agreement with the crowd. In her most solemn voice she commanded:

"Bring forth the Great Burning Pants of Shumbitt."

A Duel to the Death and Beyond

Up in the Halls of Sirrus, the twin gods were over-joyed that their gorgo experiment had finally lead to such a perfect and honourable ending.

"Hooray! Urgum's going to fight for the award after all," said Tangal.

"And when he kills Orgo, that'll remind him what being a barbarian is all about," said Tangor.

"Absolutely," said Tangal. "Once he hears that applause, there won't be any more of that softhand reward money rubbish!"

For a moment Tangor frowned and picked one of the remaining bananas off his head. He peeled it, took a bite and then asked, "Be honest, sister. Shouldn't we feel a bit bad about creating a creature just so that it can die horribly and make us feel better?"

It was an awkward question, which made them both realize they'd been rather selfish. But what could they do about it now? Besides, if they started to worry about it, they wouldn't enjoy the fight at all.

"It's a bit late to be feeling bad," said Tangal.

"So we may as well feel good about it then?" said Tangor. "That suits me just fine."

"It suits me too," said Tangal. "Thank goodness that's worked out all right."

Back in the Laplace Party Temple it wasn't quite so all right for Urgum. The Burning Pants were the most feared ordeal of all. He had known many fine and fearless savages who had been driven mad by the agonies of the Great Burning Pants, and already his bottom was as raw as a vulture's claw.

Urgum had left the stage to join Mungoid and Molly and the seven still snoring sons on one side of the room, while Orgo had gone over to the rest of the gorgos on the far side. A small Laplace footman in a green silk robe approached the Urgum table, followed by two painted slaves carrying a large sealed chest. The slaves banged the chest down in front of Urgum as the footman eyed him critically.

"Hmmm," he said, stroking his chin. "You're a big boy, aren't you?"

"So?" snapped Urgum.

"It's lucky for you these pants are so massive," said the footman. "Otherwise you wouldn't find them very comfy."

"Comfy?" said Urgum. "These are the Great Burning Pants of Shumbitt! How am I supposed to be *very comfy* with my bottom on fire?"

One of the slaves unlatched the cask and opened the lid. Molly stretched herself up to see inside. To her surprise, the cask was full to the brim with a black smelly liquid.

"That's tar," said Mungoid. "The runny stuff too. Very nasty."

The second slave shoved a long hooked stick into the liquid and pulled out a huge pair of dripping pants. Judging by the smell, they hadn't been washed since the start of time.

"Makes you wonder," said the footman holding his nose, "how many people have met their end in these pants over the years. When they started off they used to be white, you know."

"Well, they're brown now," said Mungoid. "It must be the tar that's turned them brown."

"Yes, that's one of the things that does it," agreed the footman before turning to Urgum. "Now then, sir, let's have your trousers off and get the pants on."

"Trousers off?" said Urgum. "Are you sure?"

"It's the rules," said the footman.

"Then tell *him* that," said Mungoid, pointing across to the other side of the hall where a similar chest had been delivered. Orgo was crouched down behind his table; he was obviously up to something.

"OY, ORGO!" shouted Mungoid, rising to his feet. "I hope you're not leaving your trousers on."

"Er ... no!" replied Orgo.

"Trousers off then!" shouted Mungoid, and soon the cheer was taken up by the crowd.

"Trousers OFF OFF OFF! Trousers OFF OFF OFF!"

With a defiant roar, Urgum whipped off his own trousers, then waved them round his head and slapped them on the table in front of him. Molly had clamped her eyes shut and was burning in embarrassment, but was still pleased to hear the massive cheer that rang around the hall.

"Come on then, Orgo!" shouted Urgum. "Let's see you."

Orgo glanced round uneasily, then ducked down out of sight. A moment later he reappeared and waved his own trousers in the air before slapping them down on his table. The footman beside him winked at the other gorgos, who all stood around their leader, grinning. There was obviously something going on over there...

"...but his trousers are off, so it must be fair," remarked Mungoid.

The two slaves by Urgum carefully held the pants open for him to step into.

"Oooh," said the footman seeing Urgum's red raw blisters. "Your bottom looks nasty."

"Of course it looks nasty!" snapped Urgum. "It's supposed to look nasty. It's a bottom. Now let's get on with it."

Urgum took a deep breath, then shoved his legs into the holes. With a cold sticky squelch the slaves hoisted the great pants up and fixed them in place with a pair of leather braces that went over his shoulders. As soon as the tar touched Urgum's raw skin it stung like an army of scorpions, and the vapours coming off the pants were making him feel quite sick. Mungoid approached and held out a lit candle to get a good look.

"So these are the Great Burning Pants of Shumbitt?" he said, inspecting them closely. "Phew! Just the smell's enough to kill you." At that moment the vapours from the pants caused the candle flame to flare up and spit white sparks.

"GET BACK, YOU GREAT BETTY!"

ordered Urgum. "I don't want to be roasted before the ordeal has even started."

Urgum waddled uncomfortably towards the middle of the hall to meet Orgo who had waddled over from the Gorgo table.

"Excuse me, please," came Hunjah's voice from the archway. Urgum and Orgo turned to see the little guard in his big hat trying to usher a few savages aside. "Move right over to the sides, please. We've got to keep the entrance clear so they can get to the fountain. You don't want to be in the way if they come running through."

On hearing this the last few savages immediately hurried away from the arch. They had no intention of being caught in the path of the Great Burning Pants of Shumbitt.

"If both contestants are ready," announced Mulma, "bring forth the torches."

A cheer went up from the crowd as two more slaves approached, each carrying a flaming torch. Urgum and Orgo were handed one each and stood there with their arms up in the air, keeping the flames as far away as possible from their great dripping pants. Sweat ran down their bodies.

"You know the rules," said Mulma.

They did. Each fighter had to try to set fire to the other's pants while keeping his own unlit. And once your pants were burning, how long could you take the gruesome groin-grilling agony?

"The first to run out and sit in the fountain is the

loser," declared Mulma. "Contestants, the time has come to ... ENGAGE!"

Warily, Urgum and Orgo took a few steps towards each other, flames still held high.

"Give up now, loser!" said Orgo.

"No way," said Urgum. "Prepare to have your botty barbecued."

"I don't think so," sneered Orgo and in a flash he flicked his torch down in front of him. A small glowing ember shot loose and flew straight towards Urgum's pants. Just in time, Urgum reached out and caught it in the palm of his hand, where it sizzled for a moment.

"Is that supposed to impress me?" sneered Orgo.

Urgum shook his head, then popped the ember in his mouth and crunched it in his teeth. A gasp went up from the crowd, and even Orgo couldn't think of anything clever to say. Urgum gave him a big satisfied grin and blew a tiny stream of smoke from his mouth.

Everybody in the room thought, *Wow – he's SO tough!*

Actually, Urgum didn't think that. What Urgum was thinking was, *YEE-OWWW! What did I do that for? Ucky yucky doo-dah that hurts ... EEEK! Urgum, you great steaming ninny, whatever you do, don't ever do that AGAIN.*

The crowd held its breath as the two savages circled each other. Occasionally one would move forward but the other would leap aside, usually colliding with the people standing all around the edge. The crowd would gasp or cheer or laugh, but Urgum and Orgo didn't hear them. Every little bit of their attention was focused on each other.

Urgum's instinct for survival was coming into play. Although the savages were moving round each other very cautiously, Urgum was gradually allowing himself to be backed into a corner of the hall. He didn't want to move back too quickly in case it became obvious what he was doing, but soon he was aware that right behind him was the table he'd been aiming for – a table that had a mass of burning candles on it! Suddenly he reached behind him and swept his arm across the table top and sent a shower of burning candles flying across the room. Orgo frantically threw himself around to avoid them, and as he did so his little gorgo wings fluttered and for a brief moment he rose into the air. This had given the gorgo an idea.

Orgo retreated right back from Urgum and then suddenly came running towards him, taking a jump and flapping his little wings as hard as he could. Orgo almost reached the roof of the hall and beneath him Urgum looked up in astonishment as a shower of tar from Orgo's pants fell down around him. Passing his torch down from his hand to his foot, Orgo swished it around among the falling droplets and Urgum found himself standing in a blazing rain of flame. Urgum dived to the side and slid along the floor, leaving a long back trail of tar behind him. He came to a rest with his pants smoking heavily but thankfully not yet alight. For a brief moment Orgo's laugh rang out, "ɔakka ɔakka ɔakka", but as he was looking at Urgum he forgot to concentrate on where he was going.

KLANGG!

Orgo collided with the top of the wall, dropping his torch on to a ledge immediately below him. He tried to grab on to the smooth ruby surface, but it was no use. Slowly he started to slide down. Now it was Urgum's turn to laugh as Orgo's dripping tarry pants were getting ever closer to the eager flames of his torch. The crowd underneath Orgo scattered, but then with an almighty shove he threw himself back from the wall and fluttered down to the floor. Like Urgum, his pants were smoking but not quite alight.

As Orgo struggled to his feet, Urgum saw his chance.

He lunged forwards, thrusting his torch in front of him, but Orgo just managed to throw himself aside. A few black droplets that flew from Orgo's pants were caught in the flame from Urgum's torch and immediately exploded in a shower of white sparks. Urgum didn't get out of the way quickly enough and to his horror the first yellow flickers of fire appeared on the front of his smouldering pants. Without thinking he tossed his torch aside, then spat on his hands and smothered the baby flames before they could take hold. The stinging pain from the sticky tar on his bottom was already unbearable. Urgum couldn't even begin to imagine how bad it would feel if the whole lot caught fire.

But he didn't have to imagine it, because at that moment a voice called from the crowd.

"Here, Orgo, catch!" shouted one of the gorgos. Urgum looked up to see a leather flagon of punch flying from the crowd. Orgo caught it and after gulping in a big breath he took a deep slurp. Lying between them on the floor was Urgum's blazing torch. Urgum dived to grab it, but as he did so Orgo blew out a shower of punch with all his might. The punch hit the blazing torch and turned into a massive sheet of flame that billowed across the hall straight at Urgum. Urgum's pants immediately burst into flame again and soon thick smoke was shooting down out of both leg holes.

"Ow ooh ooyah eeeek!" screamed Urgum.

"Oooooh!" gasped the crowd excitedly.

"Don't get excited everybody," shouted Molly across the room. "He's only pretending it's sore, aren't you, Dad?"

For a moment Urgum stopped and stared at Molly in utter disbelief. Then gritting his teeth, Urgum forced himself to smile and pretend that he was only pretending to be suffering powerful pangs of posteric pain.

"Thought so," yelled Molly cheerfully. "But this is no time to stand around chatting. You'd better get those flames out, Dad."

Oddly enough, Urgum had already thought of that. Frantically he leapt and rolled about the hall beating at his pants with his hands, but this only seemed to whip the flames into a greater frenzy. Orgo laughed his foul laugh: "*cakka cakka cakka.*" It would only be seconds before the fire would be causing serious damage to Urgum's bottom department. Urgum tried to tell his legs not to sprint out to the fountain of beautiful bubbling water, but it wasn't easy. All around his midriff the flames were shooting upwards and, worse still, Orgo was now holding his torch. Somehow he had to get that torch back and set fire to the gorgo's pants.

"I don't suppose you'll be needing this any more!" sneered Orgo and with a mighty throw he hurled the torch out through the archway. It flew across the courtyard with an arc of smoke trailing behind it, and landed in the fountain. Urgum groaned as he heard the quick fizzle and hiss of the extinguished flames. Now he had no way of igniting the gorgo's pants ... or had he?

Through the smoke that was shooting up past his face Urgum spotted the black trail of tar he'd made when he'd slid along the floor earlier and Orgo was standing on the far end of it. Gritting his teeth even more than before, Urgum gradually moved round to the other end of the trail.

"So tell me?" laughed Orgo. "How sore is your bottom now, Urgum?"

"If you really want to know," said Urgum. "Why don't you find out for yourself?"

So saying he suddenly sat down *whump* on the floor. OWWW! As if his bottom wasn't already sore enough ... but then just as he'd hoped, the fire from his own pants leapt on to the tar trail, shot along the floor and straight up into Orgo's pants.

"Arghhh!" screamed Orgo, trying to beat the flames

out, but it was no use. The fingers of flames had taken a tight grip on his pants and weren't going to let go.

Both savages knew it was hopeless to try and beat their pants out, so now it was just a question of endurance. With arms folded defiantly and pants ablaze, they both stood either side of the archway facing each other. Who would be the first to crack and dive through the arch into the fountain? Urgum's pants had been burning longest and already he could feel a lot of heat where he didn't want to feel a lot of heat. But what was even more worrying, Orgo didn't seem to look too worried.

"Hot enough for you?" jeered Orgo.

"Quite pleasant actually," squeaked Urgum. He hadn't

meant his voice to come out that high. By now his teeth were so gritted that he couldn't grit them any more and so he was having to grit his gums. Again Orgo laughed: "*cakka cakka cakka!*"

"We do this for fun at home," laughed Orgo. "I could stand here all day. So why not do that big bottom of yours a favour and shove it in the fountain?"

Across the courtyard Urgum could hear the water slapping lazily around the ruby pool. It was tempting, so tempting. By now he was starting to cough as the smelly fumes from his pants wafted straight up his nose.

"Having a problem, Urgum?" said Orgo.

"I'm not used to having such a rotten smell coming from my pants," said Urgum, trying to keep his voice steady. "But obviously you are."

"What???" Orgo was furious. "How dare you question the perfumed paradise that is my underwear?"

The crowd were whispering to each other excitedly. Who would be the first to crack? Urgum's pants were well ablaze, but Orgo's pants were catching up fast. Everybody settled back to watch as the smell of toasted buttocks filled the air.

At the same time as this had been going on, Molly had been puzzled.

"Klangg?" she said to herself.

"What?" asked Mungoid.

"Klangg," repeated Molly. "When Orgo hit the wall he should have gone *splatt*. Or *thudd*."

"It's *cablump*," said Mungoid. "That's the noise somebody makes when they fly through the air and hit a wall."

"*Cablump?*" asked Molly. "Are you sure?"

"Of course," insisted Mungoid. "Heard it hundreds of times. But if you don't believe me..."

Mungoid had spotted QGQQQQQ, who was crawling away under a table. He went over and grabbed him.

"Thought you'd quietly sneak off, did you?" snarled Mungoid. "And we were supposed to think you were the Savage of the Year!"

Clutching the pink poppo's ankles and spinning on his heel, Mungoid hurled QGQQQQQ around and then let go. A screaming pink blob flew over the other savages and hit the wall with a loud ...

CABLUMP!

"You're right!" said Molly. "But when Orgo hit the wall he went *klangg*!"

"That's more of a metal sound," said Mungoid.

They both looked carefully at Orgo as he stood opposite Urgum. His pants were spluttering and sizzling away, but he was still managing to keep a smug look on his face.

"Oh no, I've just realized," exclaimed Molly. "Orgo's wearing metal underpants!"

"Do you think so?" gasped Mungoid.

"If someone was wearing metal pants, what noise would they make when they hit a wall?"

"**KLANGG**!" they both agreed.

"He must have kept them on when he took his trousers off," said Molly. "And metal pants wouldn't burn!"

"True," said Mungoid. "They'd heat up eventually, but it would give him a lot more time. Poor old Urgum!"

"Don't panic, Mungoid," Molly's face was alight with excitement. "If Orgo's wearing metal pants, *we've got him*." She ran across the hall to Urgum. "DAD!" she cried. "It's all right, you can go to the fountain!"

"No!" shouted Urgum in a very squeaky voice. "Never! I'll lose."

"Trust me," said Molly. "Do it!"

By now Urgum's eyes were streaming with tears from the pain and the smoke. His knees were starting to buckle, and he slumped on to all fours. Molly reached through the smoke and took his hand. Flames licked up her arm, Urgum tried to shake her off but she wouldn't let go.

"Come on," she cried. "I'm not leaving you. Come through to the water."

Molly heaved with all her might and very slowly dragged Urgum through the archway. Behind them the chorus of boos and jeers was deafening.

"You may as well do as she says," taunted Orgo. "Let's face it, you just can't take the pain."

Molly turned back and screamed at Orgo crossly through the arch.

"You stay back! I'm not having you follow us just so you can laugh."

"Oh really?" replied Orgo. "Well, maybe you can boss Daddy around but you can't tell me what to do. I'm coming out to see the great Urgum's burning botty."

Orgo stepped under the archway, but as soon as he did so his bottom started to twitch uncontrollably. With a cry of dismay Orgo realized he had been tricked.

Looking up he saw the mass of swords, axes, mallets and other metal objects stuck to the ceiling.

Very slowly his feet left the floor and his bottom rose up in the air, leaving his head and arms dangling down. Orgo realized that his secret metal pants were being dragged upwards by the invisible force of the lodestone. In desperation he stretched out for something to cling on to just as Hunjah was hurrying into the archway to try and stop everyone else charging through. Orgo grabbed the big guard hat on Hunjah's head, taking Hunjah completely by surprise.

But Hunjah wasn't nearly as surprised as Orgo. Hunjah's head came away from his body and Orgo continued rising towards the ceiling, holding the head out in front of him. The crowd in the hall were all pushing forwards to see. Some laughed, some jeered, some whistled, but most just stood there amazed. It wasn't every day that you saw a pukey-green half-budgie half-gorilla savage floating around with its bottom shooting flames and talking to a severed head in a big guard hat.

"You're disqualified," sniffed Hunjah crossly.

In shock, Orgo let go of the head, but then without the extra weight to hold him down he started rising faster and faster until...

KLANGG! As Orgo's flaming bottom collided with the ceiling, he was stabbed, cut, walloped and smashed against all the nasty metal objects already up there. Everybody stared at his battered and bleeding body in horror until it disappeared in a thick cloud of steam coming from the fountain.

"Ahhhhhhhhhhhh!"

sighed Urgum as the cool water soaked into his innermost cavities. "That's better."

The Gloating chamber

Urgum's bottom was wrapped in a very, very big bandage that dripped with cooling lotion. A few wisps of smoke were still wafting up from the back, and although his face shuddered with pain, it couldn't disguise his joy as he walked down the ruby-walled passageway. Holding the golden statuette out in front of him, he stepped through the heavy black curtain. Molly was about to follow when Mungoid stopped her. He stood across the entrance and folded his arms, making it clear to anybody else that they wouldn't get in either.

"Sorry, Molly, you're not allowed in."

"Oh?" said Molly. "So what goes on in there?"

"It's the Gloating Chamber," said Mungoid. "It's where they put the losers to die after a duel. Orgo's in there now, and the only other person allowed in is the victor. What happens between them is absolutely secret."

"Why?"

"Oh, it's the best bit of winning a duel," said Mungoid. "Urgum will be waving his Savvy in Orgo's face and having a real laugh."

"Charming," said Molly, trying to peer around Mungoid and through the gap in the curtains. "Still, Dad deserves it. He's been so miserable, it'd be nice to see him jolly up a bit."

Mungoid thought about this, then glanced up and down the corridor. "Well, seeing as you helped …" he said. "Just slip in very quietly and stay behind the curtain so they don't see you. Shhh!"

So Molly slipped in.

Laid out on a ruby slab was Orgo the Gorgo. His body was covered in a velvet blanket with just his head sticking from the top. He was staring sadly into space, trying to think of some famous last words. Urgum was leaning over him with a huge grin on his face.

"Hah!" said Urgum. "You don't look so mighty now, Orgo! Serves you right, you and your metal pants."

"I know," groaned Orgo. "You won. Well done."

"Yeah I did," agreed Urgum, leering down at the

strange beaked head. He whipped away the blanket and a few blood-matted green feathers fluttered to the ground, all droopy and broken. "So what have you got to say for yourself with your big feety hands and your silly little wings?"

"What's to say?" said Orgo, his face twisting in pain. "I was beaten by the fiercest savage in the Lost Desert."

"Too right," said Urgum, holding the golden statuette in the air and marching around beating his chest. "So I won and YOU lost."

"Yes," said Orgo.

Urgum's mouth was still grinning, but his eyes were starting to look uncomfortable.

"Then I'm better than you, so why don't you just admit it?" he demanded.

"I admit it," said Orgo.

Urgum stomped away, then span back crossly. "Look, you're not doing this right. When I say *admit it* you're meant to say *NEVER!* and then add something like, *I've got a thousand brothers who are coming for you*, then I can say, *Pah! Bring 'em on, I could use a laugh*, and then you curse me with your dying breath and so on."

"Well, I haven't got a thousand brothers," said Orgo. "There's just me."

"Well, even so, I thought you'd die with more style. This is rubbish! Anyone would think you're scared."

Orgo didn't answer, he just gritted his beak and groaned.

"Hey," said Urgum. "I said you're SCARED! Well?"

"I am," said Orgo.

Urgum was aghast. "Really? Scared of dying? But you've been the best enemy I've ever had. Don't let me down now!"

"Wouldn't you be scared of dying?"

"Me? Hah! I laugh in the face of death. I chortle at the thought of kicking the bucket. I wet my pants at the very idea of stepping one beyond. Death? It's just an invitation to join my barbarian gods, Tangor and Tangal. When I die, I'll be sitting between them eating divine nectar for eternity. YUM! So what are your plans?"

"Nothing," said Orgo.

"But won't your gods be pleased to see you?" asked Urgum. "They should be, you were a great fighter. Not as great as me of course, but still great."

"I never had gods," said Orgo.

"Rubbish! Everybody's got gods," said Urgum. "What gods did your family have?"

"Family?"

"Your tribe then? What did you have in the old days?"

"I never had old days. I just arrived on my own. I'm just a joke, an experiment. Just like the other little gorgos, and the poppo."

"The poppo!" smiled Urgum. "Most savages would have just eaten it, but you treated it like a mate and even tried to get an award for it. You've got real class! Surely you've got something lined up for when you're dead?"

"Nothing."

"Ooh, that's creepy," said Urgum, looking into the

gorgo's sad black eyes. "So this is really it for you? No more banging mirrors or bananas? Seems a bit unfair when you've been so good."

Orgo coughed and shivered, and his black tongue flopped out of the side of his beak. Urgum reached down for the velvet blanket and put it back over him again. "By the way, to be honest, I think your feet are great. Climbing, holding extra weapons, eating faster … maybe I'll pray to my gods and see if they can sort some out for me."

"I wish I had gods," said Orgo.

"Yeah, well, having decent gods isn't easy. I've got to work at it," said Urgum, polishing his little golden statue with a corner of the blanket. "I've got to be tough and merciless and fierce and all that."

"That's what I was trying to do," said Orgo.

"You did it well, too!" said Urgum. "You'd have made a great barbarian."

"Thanks," said Orgo. "And that divine nectar sounds good, but it's too late now."

Slowly the gorgo's eyelids started to close. Urgum watched him, then looked at the award, then looked back again.

"No!" said Urgum. "It's not too late."

Urgum tugged back the blanket and laid the golden statuette on Orgo's chest, then folded the gorgo's long arms over it. "You hang on to that. That proves you deserve to be a barbarian, and my gods will be honoured to feed you divine nectar for eternity."

"Don't you need it?"

"Me? Nah! My gods know who I am, I'm the fiercest savage the Lost Desert has ever known. And besides, they're not expecting me for a long time yet."

The gorgo clutched his arms tight around the little gold figure, the pain slipped from his face and he let out a long, long final sigh. Urgum closed the pink eyelids down with his fingertips, then looked upwards. "Make sure you take good care of him," he said.

Urgum stepped back out of the black curtains and poked Mungoid in the ribs.

"Eeek!" said Mungoid.

"That's that," he said. "He's gone."

"Feeling better now?" asked Mungoid.

Urgum thought about it, then nodded. "A lot better!"

"Hey," said Mungoid, seeing Urgum's empty hands. "Where's the … eeek!" Mungoid, just had a second poke in the ribs. He looked round to find Molly behind him with her finger to her lips and shaking her head.

"Pardon?" asked Urgum. "You said, *Where's the eek?*"

"Sorry," said Mungoid. "I was forgetting, whatever happens in the Gloating Chamber is absolutely secret."

"Dead right," said Urgum. "Nobody must ever know what I did in there, so don't ever ask me again or I'll kill you with a lot of lethal death."

Mungoid nodded solemnly to show he respected Urgum's wishes. Then Urgum nodded solemnly to show he trusted Mungoid. Then Mungoid nodded solemnly to show he trusted Urgum to trust him, and then Urgum nodded solemnly to show that he respected the trust that Mungoid had in him to trust him and by then Molly had got bored.

"Come on, boys," she said, taking them both by the hand. "It's been a long day. Time to go home."

Bedtime for All Good Savages

It was a good job Molly knew the password, because by the time they had all ridden back to Golgarth Cragg, she was the only one left awake. Even the thin moon could hardly be bothered to shine, probably because it was going through that embarrassing phase where it was the same shape as a toenail clipping. As the horses all plodded wearily down Smiley Alley, the great Guardian of Golgarth stirred.

"PASSWORD," boomed Olk's voice.

"Shhh!" said Molly, pointing at the others. Mungoid was snoring on the back of his ox, the first proper sleep he'd had since he'd pulled Abill out of his well. The boys were still groggy from the effects of the punch and Urgum was so tired he hadn't noticed that he had fallen off his horse ages ago and the beast had been kicking him the rest of the way home.

"Sorry," said Olk. The great blade twitched in embarrassment. "… *password* …?"

"Enormous strawberry fool ice cream," said Molly, and in they all went.

Mungoid's ox ambled away to the ungoid cave, and the boys all flumped off their horses and fell asleep in a heap on the ground. Molly got off her horse and then got Urgum's horse to give him a final kick into their cave. It woke him up just enough for Molly to pull his arm around her shoulders and guide him down the dark passageway that lead to his bedroom, where friendly candlelight was shining out through the archway.

"Is that you, dear?" came Divina's voice.

Molly staggered in and Divina leapt up from her dressing table to help shuffle Urgum towards the bed. With a final shove, his knees hit the side and he was asleep before he'd even collapsed on to the sheets. Divina went to sit down again and look smugly at a nice big gap she'd arranged in the middle of all her bottles and bits. The golden Savvy statuette was going to look just *so* neat there!

"Well?" asked Divina excitedly. "Where is it?"

"He hasn't got it," said Molly.

"Hasn't …" blurted Divina. "… *got it*? But I thought …"

"It's a long story."

"Oh, poor Urgie," said Divina. "He so wanted to be the winner."

"Oh, but he was the best winner ever!" said Molly, wishing she could tell the whole story but not daring to as she didn't really want to be killed with a lot of lethal death. "He'll just be disappointed he didn't bring you anything to put on your dressing table."

A huge contented snore came from the bed.

"He doesn't sound very disappointed," said Divina, looking at Urgum crossly.

"Good," said Molly.

Neither of them noticed a little creature hop in through the door. A couple more hops and it was on the dressing table. It took a *deeep* breath, then put its feet in its mouth and went to sleep.

"Trust me, Mum," yawned Molly. "We don't need awards here so long as we've got Dad."

"Well, yes, I know that," said Divina. "But I can't exactly use your father to fill a gap on my dressing table, can I?"

"Gap?" asked Molly, rubbing her eyes sleepily and heading off to her own room. "What gap?"

Molly had gone, so Divina looked at her dressing table again. How very odd! There *was* a gap there, but now ...? The bedroom rocked gently with the sound of another big snore. It was a long relaxed untroubled safe warm friendly snore that completely filled everything and didn't leave *any* gaps. Divina sighed happily. Molly was right.

They didn't need awards or anything else, not when they had Urgum the Axeman.

The Epilogue:
Eternal Nectar

Up in the Halls of Sirrus the divine twins gasped as the hulking figure with the beak and the perfectly brilliant green feathers strode in through their doorway on its feet-hands. It had learnt to assert itself since it first appeared as a little thing on their table, and in the spirit world of Sirrus, that had made it a lot bigger. "Urgum sent me," it said, holding out a small golden statue.

"We know!" said Tangor.

"And you're expecting divine nectar for ever?" asked Tangal.

"That'll do for starters," said Orgo.

Tangor and Tangal exchanged anxious glances. They

hadn't planned on this, but in their hearts they knew it served them right. Orgo was their creature, he'd done exactly what he was supposed to do and he was entitled to be rewarded for it.

"You better make yourself comfortable then," said Tangor. "We'll get some nectar ready."

As Tangal went to open a tin of divine nectar, Orgo plonked himself in the biggest chair and shifted around until he was absolutely and totally comfortable. After all, he was going to be sitting there for eternity, which was a very long time.

"I'll get you a spoon," said Tangor.

Orgo grinned and held up both hands.

"OK, two spoons," said Tangor.

Orgo held up his feet-hands too.

"Not … four spoons?" gasped Tangor.

Orgo grinned and nodded. Tangor cursed mightily and went to rummage in the spoons drawer as Tangal opened several more tins of divine nectar. For Orgo, eternity was going to be a very long time. But for the gods it was going to seem like a very very *very* long time.